BLOOD MOON

THE GODDESS CHRONICLES BOOK TWO

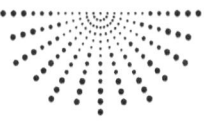

KB ANNE

Published by Gripping Tales, LLC, Pennsylvania.

ISBN: 978-1-956915-01-3

Cover Design by Anika Willmans, Ravenborn Covers

Editorial Services by Laura Parnum, Laura Parnum Books

❀ Created with Vellum

To my readers,

KICK ASS.
You got this.
~K

JOIN THE KOVEN

Read Clarissa and Carman's origin story, The Druids Sisters of the Gallicennial, FREE by signing up for K's Koven. Be the FIRST to find out about new releases from Best-Selling Author, K.B. Anne. PLUS, receive Newsletter Subscriber Only Bonus Content, insight on Celtic Mythology, Druids, Witches, Werewolves, and Magic, and so much more! Join K's Koven today!

PROLOGUE

J've tempted fate one too many times not to be surprised as the killer stalks toward me, but still I am. An ocean separated us. An *ocean* for god's sake. But still he's here. Ready to rip out my throat.

~Gigi Brennan, BLOOD MOON: THE GODDESS
CHRONICLES BOOK TWO

HANGING FROM THE GALLOWS

*M*y best friend is dead. Dead. It doesn't seem possible that the world continues to rotate around the sun without her in it. It certainly isn't fair that I continue breathing while she gets shoved into a coffin and dropped into the ground.

How did I, Gigi Brennan, release Clayone, the Original Werewolf?

Oh, that's right, because Gram and Uncle Mark—or really "Dad"—believe I'm the Celtic Goddess Brigit reincarnated.

The last time I checked, goddesses don't break into their neighbors' houses, or lie to the school principal on a daily basis or, well, suck the tonsils out of anyone with a pulse.

Do gods and goddesses even kiss? Zeus went far beyond lip locking with mortals. Ever hear the term "demigod"? Zeus had armies of them. But he's a Greek god. Are Celtic gods and goddesses just as horny as him?

Though, honestly, being Brigit is the least of my worries.

The moment Lizzie stopped breathing, I stopped breathing. I stopped believing in everything and everyone. The lies

Gram and Uncle Mark told me confirm that the world has gone insane. That it's a world not worth living in anymore.

A world I don't want to live in anymore.

Knock. Knock.

"Gigi, honey?" Gram calls out from the other side of the door. "Some officers are here, and they'd like to speak with you and Scott about what happened up at the church."

Do I even know what happened? It feels like a bad trip, and one I don't want to repeat.

"I'm not talking to anyone," I mutter into my pillow.

The door clicks open, and she walks in. "Dear, you have to talk to them."

The mind-reading stuff is really a pain in the ass, especially when it's my own grandmother reading my freaking mind.

I flip over to face away from her. "I don't want to."

The bed moves as she sits down next to me. Her presence alone calms me more than any tea or smell ever could.

"Gi, you owe it to your friends to make sure no one else goes up there and gets injured. Or worse."

I stare at the wolf statue on my nightstand. Wolves are innocent. Pure. Good. How could someone turn them into a killing machine?

"I don't even know what to tell them."

Scott's the storyteller. He's the entertainer. He's the good one.

"You will," she says.

She's always given me far too much credit. Credit I do not deserve.

"You do deserve it, Gigi. You do."

THE CLIMB DOWN THE STAIRS FEELS LIKE I'M APPROACHING THE gallows. Not that the thought didn't already cross my mind, but Gram, Scott, and Dad shouldn't have to endure my death. The longer I live, the more I'll suffer, and I should suffer for what I've done.

When I enter the living room, I see Scott leaning against the wall and Dad standing at the door in quiet conversation with the two officers. In my heart, I know it's right to call him "Dad." He's always been there for me, always watched out for me. Just like Scott. We might now officially, or at least metaphysically, be related by blood, but they have always been my people. They are my family, and I will do everything in my power to protect them.

"Gigi, Scott, this is Officer Lamberton and Officer Smith. They'd like to talk to you about what happened yesterday. Shall we?" Dad says, gesturing to the sofas. The same sofas we passed out on last night. The same sofas where we discovered the shocking truth that I unleashed the evilest werewolf of all time. A werewolf who bit Ryan and killed Lizzie. A werewolf who will kill anyone who comes near the church in order to feed. In order to gain strength. In order to kill me. I don't fear for my own life, but I fear for Gram, Scott, and Dad. I fear for these officers.

"We've already been to the hospital to talk to Ryan," Officer Smith says.

I recognize him. He's Tom's dad. Tom plays football with Scott and Ryan.

The flame of possibility blooms within me. "He's conscious?"

"He is, but he's completely delusional. His version of the events yesterday is pretty outrageous. He claims some type of beast attacked the two of them. We're hoping you two can help us figure out what we're going up against when we go up there."

I raise my hand. "That won't be necessary."

Everyone turns to me, and unfortunately, I know what they're thinking. I know what they're all thinking.

"It won't be necessary to go up to the church. There isn't anything there."

"Gi?" Scott says. He wants to tell them everything. Every last stinking detail.

Don't.

His forehead bulges, but he keeps his mouth shut.

"We were camping in the woods Saturday night, and we were telling ghost stories. We decided to hike up to the old church the next day. When we got there, we were messing around, trying to scare each other. It was dark inside, and it was covered with cobwebs. Then all of a sudden the floor collapsed and Lizzie and Ryan fell down to the basement or something. Everyone was screaming. Ryan lifted Lizzie, and Scott and I pulled her up the rest of the way. Blood was everywhere."

I babble on and on, unable to stop. Knowing if I do stop, even for a breath, I won't be able to continue.

"Then we pulled Ryan up. As soon as he was out of the hole, Scott lifted Lizzie, and we ran out of the place as fast as we could. We were so scared. When we were far away from the church, we finally stopped. That's when I cleaned Ryan's cut and bandaged him. I tried to find a pulse on Lizzie, but she was already . . . she was already . . ." A wave of sobs removes my power of speech.

Scott wraps his arm around me, immediately calming me. "When we got them out of the woods, we drove to the hospital, but it was too late for Lizzie," he says.

"Ryan said they were attacked by some type of beast," Officer Lamberton says. "Do you know what he's talking about?"

Unfortunately, I know exactly what he's talking about.

"The building was really old, and the floor was covered in animal droppings. A rat probably bit him when he fell."

A freaking giant rat.

I cringe at the memory of Ryan's blood-curdling scream. If someone lights a match near my mouth, I will burst into flames.

Lamberton's eyes shine as he caresses his holstered gun. "You're sure there's no rabid animal we need to hunt down?"

The young cop seems to possess a fetish for his shiny weapon. A deadly instrument that, if past crimes in Vernal Falls are any indication, will never need to be used in the line of duty. Scott and I nod our heads in agreement.

They buy our story hook, line, and bullshit.

Officer Smith stands up with Officer Lamberton following. "Appreciate your time. We've got everything we need. If we have more questions, we'll give you a call."

Dad shakes each of their hands. "Thank you, gentlemen."

"Ma'am," they say together, nodding at Gram before Dad closes the door behind them.

Gram wraps her arm around me. "You did great, Gigi. I knew you would."

Dad agrees with her, but there is one person in the room who is not in agreement.

"Why didn't you tell them the truth? Why did you lie to them? They're going to think Ryan's a complete nutjob now."

Dad crouches down in front of us. "Scott, that's enough. Gi did the right thing. If you told them what really happened, do you think they'd believe you anyway? And what would happen to them if they went up to the church?"

Before Scott can answer, Dad continues. "They would be killed. Clayone would feed on them and grow stronger with every death. Right now, he's trapped in the church until the next full moon. That evening, he'll be able to leave his prison to feed. When he builds enough strength, he will come here.

7

The spells we have in place and the others we will cast should keep him out, but in just over a month, he will be more powerful than he has been in a thousand years."

"Why's that?" Scott asks quietly.

"On October 31, the eve of Samhain, there will be a Super Blue Blood Moon during the lunar eclipse. The strong oak doors of this house and the enchantments placed upon it may not be enough to protect any of us," Dad whispers.

Shit. What have I done?

INSERT FOOT IN MOUTH

*A*s we walk into the hospital, the unnatural stench of bleach and sickness slams into our nostrils like a freaking herd of football players at an all-you-can-eat buffet. I don't understand how the world can continue moving forward without Lizzie in it.

"So, what do we tell Ryan when we see him? Do we lie to him too?"

He's still mad at me for lying to the police. If he only knew about the searing pain in my throat every time I lie, he might be more sympathetic. Then again, I don't want his sympathy. I don't want anyone's sympathy. My best friend is freaking dead, and I killed her.

"Scott, you know it was for his own good. He can't know what really happened, and we can't provide Clayone with a free meal ticket. I can't kill anyone else."

Nurses, doctors scurry past us, moving from patient to patient, trying to help the ones they can. But what happens to the ones they can't save?

"It wasn't just you. I'm the one who told that stupid story.

I'm the one who gave everyone the idea to sneak into the church."

I'm about to argue with him until I realize that we're standing in front of Ryan's room. My plan to remain upbeat and cheerful fails miserably when confronted with Ryan's limp form. He's always been the strong one. The one who saved me from being completely alone while I waited for my daily session with Principal Donahue. The one who saw past the freak beside him. Someone who didn't know the Gigi of the past, who wasn't related to me, but still sought my company and became my friend. To see him so weak and frail makes me reevaluate my own humanity. Because, of everything I learned over the past few days, I am human. A mortal, very breakable human.

Fortunately, Scott, with his never-ending optimism and ability to shoot the bull even in the most difficult circumstances, manages to fill the void. "Hey, Ryan, you look like you were run over by an angry line of defenders."

Ryan laughs weakly. He wants to joke. He wants to banter back and forth with Scott, but he's got only one person on his mind. "How is she? No one will tell me how she is."

And just like that, without a word or a nod, we're at his side, each taking a hand.

"She's no longer with us," I whisper.

"She will be forever young in our hearts and minds. She will watch over you always, guiding you when you need her the most," Scott adds.

Ryan leans his head back against the pillows and closes his eyes. No longer needing to keep our emotions in check— no longer caring period—we weep for our lost friend. We weep for all we have lost, and our losses have been catastrophic.

"I love her with all my heart," he moans.

"You'll be with her soon," I reassure him.

He closes his eyes and falls into a peaceful sleep. My words give him comfort, and I am thankful I could give him that. After several long minutes of watching him, Scott tilts his head to the door. He needs to speak to me outside in private, because he's pissed.

As soon as we're in the hall, he turns to me, his face angry and full of rage. "What the hell was that about?"

"What?"

"'You'll be with her soon?' You basically told him he's going to die. The doctors all say he's improving. We need to boost his spirit, not knock him down. He is not going to die!" he shouts before storming off down the corridor, leaving a trail of people staring from him to me.

I watch him leave, not really sure what I did or why Scott got so upset about it. I know Ryan is his best friend. I'd never want to hurt either one of them, but what I said felt true. What I said is true.

But that doesn't mean I should have said it. I just told my brother's best friend, and one of my best friends, he's going to die . . .

I am a fucking asshole.

3
WEREWOLF NIBBLES

*S*cott left me at the hospital. Granted it was warranted—I am an asshole and deserve to walk the three miles home after what I said to Ryan. For the first time in days I am truly by myself, and I realize how alone I really am. No Lizzie. No Scott. No Ryan. Not even Breas. Not that I can stand him or want his company, but with him around I wouldn't be completely alone. No doubt he'll show up tonight when we're in the throes of an intense family game of "Name That Goddess." He'll waltz in, acting like he didn't disappear for a few days, and beg forgiveness from Dad—which he'll get. Because both father and son suffer from "all-shall-be-forgiven syndrome," no matter how much of an asshole the person has been. Breas will grovel for a place to stay and promise he won't pull another disappearing act. He'll flirt with me, and because I am an idiot and weak and enjoy torturing myself, I will fall for his shenanigans again.

In a way, it's his fault that Lizzie died. If he hadn't disappeared, he'd have gone camping with us, even if it was against my wishes. We still would have sat around the campfire telling ghost stories, but he would have told stories too. Stories of Ireland and the life he left behind. He would have charmed me with his false flattery. I would have hooked up with him early in the evening, because I am an asshole and wouldn't care if my friends were watching. Scott would never have told the story about the church, we would never have gone searching for it, I wouldn't have accidently released the Original Werewolf, and most important of all, Lizzie would still be alive and Ryan wouldn't have been bitten.

I stop dead in my tracks. He was bitten by a werewolf. And not just any werewolf—the Original Werewolf. I sprint the rest of the way home like my life depends on it, because I know Ryan's does.

"GRAM? DAD?" I SHOUT, RUNNING INTO THE HOUSE. WHEN NO one answers I rush through the kitchen and out the back door to the garden and greenhouse, the only places Gram goes when she's not inside. I dash down the lily-lined stone path. The lush gardens to the left and right beckon me to enter and investigate the day's growth, but more pressing issues require my attention.

As soon as I round the corner, Gram knows something's wrong. Not only is she a mind reader, but the blotches on my cheeks are a dead giveaway.

"Gi, child, are you all right? What's the matter?"

"Will Ryan—" I huff, "—turn into a werewolf?"

She pats the bench she's sitting on, the bench we've sat on a thousand times together. "Dear, sit and take a deep breath first."

I clutch my sides. "Will Ryan turn into a werewolf?"

She pats the seat again.

When I don't oblige her, she sighs. "I don't know."

13

"In the movies, every time a person gets bitten by a were-wolf and doesn't die, he turns into one."

She breathes in and out through her nose. "The legends state the same, but what you used on the wound may stop the change from taking place."

"Is that what you and Dad were talking about when you came home from the hospital?"

She nods.

"So, you really believe that I am the Goddess Brigit, don't you?"

"With all my being, and that's why I can honestly say I don't know what's going to happen to Ryan. There are no legends we're aware of that mention the magical powers of Brigit in human form."

I cross my arms. This conversation took a ghastly turn. "Gram, I am not Brigit. I have no magical powers whatsoever."

"Child, you possess more magic than anyone I've ever met, and I've known a lot of witches in my time."

"Yeah right."

"Do you think just anyone would know what herbs to use to help Ryan?"

"I used what was nearby. Besides, you taught me about them."

"No, I didn't. There are no coincidences. You stopped at that particular spot in the woods because you knew those herbs were there."

"Gram, there was blood pouring out of his neck, and Scott was about to collapse with exhaustion with Lizzie on his back. We had to stop."

"Those herbs only grow in certain areas with very specific growing conditions. If you stopped a few minutes before or after, you would have missed them."

I shake my head back and forth. This side detour has gone on far too long. She's not making any sense.

"All right," she says, "then can you explain how you found Scott when he fell in the well?"

I throw my hands up in the air. "I guessed. I knew where the well was. Besides, Scott's such a klutz."

"Gigi, you were seven years old. You were never permitted out of the backyard except when you went to school. You had never been out to the Miller's farm. You had no way of knowing the well was there." She watches my jaw set stubbornly, as I cross my arms. "Do you think other sixteen-year-olds have injured stray animals show up routinely at their doorsteps and have the ability to heal them or possess such an extensive knowledge of plants?"

"Gram, you taught me everything."

"No, I didn't. You *know* it. Brigit is the Goddess of Fertility and Harvest. Her mere presence encourages abundant growth. Before you were born, your mother and I had a small vegetable garden. We grew some tomatoes, a little lettuce, a bunch of zucchini, but not much else. After your birth, our gardens blossomed into what they are today. In fact, everyone in the neighborhood remembers back to the days when their gardens produced nothing, and now look at them!" She stands up, sweeping her arms over the lush foliage on either side of her. "Look. Look at the fertility sprung forth from Brigit. Do you think most people grow enough food to feed their families for an entire year?" She points at a giant pumpkin that snuck out of its bed, then the spiraling edamame and bean vines, the overflowing Swiss chard patch, and the fruit trees heavy with apples, pears, and peaches even though it's past their season.

"Gram, people just learn over time. They get better at it. I had nothing to do with it."

"Do other people have roses and flowers this late into the year?"

"The roses are in the greenhouse, and the fall's been warm. The plants are just confused."

She collapses back into her seat. "Child, what can I say to convince you?"

"Gram, I gotta be honest. I don't think I'll ever be convinced. I can believe Scott's my brother, because no one else can drive me that crazy. Uncle Mark as my 'biological father'? Sure. But everything else . . . I don't know. It's pretty unbelievable. I mean witches, reincarnated gods and goddesses, and magic? Come on. Why do you believe it?"

"Because Brigit selected me to serve as her voice."

If anyone else had said that to me, I'd call them nuts or worse. Probably worse. Definitely worse. Then I'd shove them out of the way, kick their ass, and get on with my life. But with Gram . . . well, she's always been a steady, reasonable voice, who maybe didn't discipline me as harshly as I deserved but was always there for me. She's always there for her circle of family and friends.

"What do you mean she 'selected you'?"

"Brigit calls to many women, but not all choose to listen. She bestows on her chosen sisters gifts. Some possess the ability to heal animals and people. Others, the gift of storytelling. Farmers, quilters, potters, and jewelry makers are all gifted from Brigit. Her most gifted read minds and project their thoughts into other's minds and often possess the gift of prophecy."

I realize these are the gifts Darius referred to at the flea market last week. He said Gram possessed many gifts, and he suspected I did too. I dismissed my own gifts, but I knew Gram was something special.

"What gifts are you gifted with?"

She winks at me. *You know.*

I clear my throat. "Gram, what gifts were you given?"

Girl, you are stubborn. She shakes her head. "As the direct descendants of Brigit, we possess all her gifts, including that of prophecy."

"Crystal balls, creepy music, and tea leaves at the bottom of a mug in a very Harry Potter-esque attic setting?"

"Not so scripted as fiction and far removed from witch books. For us, it comes in the form of a flashback, or a flash-forward, if you will. A thought or idea that takes root and blooms into something that is truth. I was sixteen when I spoke the prophecy of the next coming of Brigit. It was the most powerful prophecy I had ever given or ever would give."

"You were my age. No one ever believes a word I say. Why would anyone believe you?"

She grasps my hand. "Gi, people do believe you. You don't believe in yourself. That's where the difference lies. I had begun my training in the Order of Brigit a year earlier. As a descendant from the line, I had already given many prophecies or insights into what the future held. Some predictions were very basic, such as a particular cow giving birth on a particular day. Others were more overarching, such as predictions about the weather and the harvest. I predicted with such regularity and accuracy, that whatever I prophesized was recorded. When Brigit's next reincarnation came to me, everyone listened. Part of it was that people believed in my ability, but they also wanted to believe that Brigit desired to live with them. The problem with prophecies is that there aren't always exact dates. They can occur years, or in this case, decades into the future—that's why they're recorded."

"What is the Order of Brigit?"

"The Order of Brigit is composed of women who choose to follow the Goddess for their life. Similar to a nun or priest, but not so rigid and unforgiving, and the training is far longer than in modern religions. Women who follow the Goddess spend the first ten years in training, the next ten years in practice, and the last ten years training the next generation."

"Are you still with the Order?"

"I still worship and follow the Goddess, but I am no longer a member of the Order."

"What happened? Did you age out?"

"For twenty-three years, I was a dedicated follower of Brigit. I saw no reason why I wouldn't continue my service for another seven. But Brigit had other plans for me, and I didn't see my own future. A man visited our coven. He had traveled the world and studied many different forms of magic. He was fascinated by the vows women take to worship Brigit. We spent countless hours together, talking, laughing, falling in love, though we never spoke the words . . .

"That spring, the High Priest was away, so he stood in for him during the Beltane ritual. The same ritual at which you were conceived years later."

I swallow. There's really no need for Gram to share all the details with me. Especially the words, "intercourse" and "grandmother" spoken in the same sentence. It's bad enough I'd heard about my mom and dad.

"Nine months later, your mom and Calliope were born, and so ended my time as a follower of the Order of Brigit."

"Why did you leave the Order?"

"Mothers, while adored and appreciated by the Order, can no longer give Brigit the singular focus she requires of Order followers. She wants them to honor her by being a dedicated mother to their children. To grow a new generation of believers."

"What happened to the guy?" I can't recall a single picture of an unknown man with my grandmother.

"He left soon after the ritual."

"Why? I thought you were in love."

She smiles more to herself than me. "We were, but we were fervently dedicated to our causes. He left not knowing I was pregnant."

"Did you try to contact him?"

She shrugs her shoulders. "His plane went down somewhere over the Atlantic on his way back to Ireland."

I cradle her hands in mine. The love Gram gives rivals no one else's, and it is without condition. For her to lose someone of such importance had to be devastating. Then to lose her own daughter . . . She sacrificed so much for no end, because I am not who she believes me to be.

"Gram, I'm so sorry."

"Don't be. I had two beautiful daughters who filled my heart with love. And I have a wonderful granddaughter who is a goddess."

For once I keep my mouth shut and don't disagree with her. I really don't need to.

She can read my mind anyway.

4

GENETICS GONE WILD

There's so much I want to ask, so much I want to talk about, but there is one person who hurt the people I love, and I want to know her truth.

"Gram, what happened to Calliope? Why did she betray you and Mom?"

The words "Mom" and "Dad" roll off my tongue much easier than I anticipated. As if I had been waiting my entire life for the opportunity to use those descriptors.

"There are two types of twins. Identical, when they share the same egg, and fraternal, when two eggs grow in the same uterus. Your mom and her sister were genetically identical twins, but in every aspect—from thought to action—they were polar opposites. Lulu was the light. Calliope was the darkness. What truly set them apart was the blessing of gifts from Brigit. As I told you, most women from Brigit's line are born with a special gift—divination, the ability to heal, the ability to teach. Calliope wasn't blessed with any. Lulu possessed multiple gifts. Your mom read minds and projected her thoughts, like we do with each other. She could also see the future, like I did."

"You don't anymore?"

"No, once I became pregnant, I lost my gift. When I discovered I was having twins, I thought my love and light prophecy applied to them. Their birthdays were January 30, close to Brigit's day, but I soon realized I was wrong. There was no love in Calliope. No light. It's terrible to say that of your own daughter, but it's true. I feared her jealousy would one day consume her.

"The girls joined the Order of Brigit when they were fifteen. When Lulu was twenty, she had a vision that she would have a daughter who was Brigit. Though I no longer possessed the gift of sight, I knew it was true. A day or two later, Calliope said she had a vision that she was going to give birth to a god as well. No one recorded the prophecy. Not one person believed her. She was furious and left the Order. We didn't hear from her for several years. Then out of nowhere, she moved back with her new husband, Mark. She was a few months pregnant with Scott and finally seemed at peace with herself and the world. But all that changed once Mark met your mom. To say sparks flew between them would be a gross understatement, so they purposefully stayed apart. Neither one wanted to hurt Calliope. But living in the same town and belonging to the same coven made it a constant struggle to keep their distance from each other. Sabbats came and went that year, and Beltane was fast approaching. Mark became the High Priest, and at Calliope's pushing, the coven decided to carry out the traditional worship ritual. You already know what happened that night, but I didn't tell you about the magic of the evening. Everyone present truly believed that the God and Goddess blessed us with their presence that night.

"A few months later Scott was born. The older he got, the more withdrawn and forlorn Calliope became. All the love and light she had exuded for months when she was pregnant began to vanish. Then, when your mom discovered she was pregnant, things went from bad to much, much worse.

"When you were born everyone scrutinized your movements, your cries, and your tears. You didn't cry often, but when you did, the tears were collected for blessings."

Little did everyone know that when I cry it's like battery acid. Unless they want to start a car, they're better off using distilled water.

"The ever-present question lingered. Is she, or isn't she?"

She isn't.

"At the same time, not one person even considered that Scott was a god. Most of us forgot about the prophecy because it wasn't even recorded. It was so easy for us to dismiss Calliope's words because of the timing of it and her jealous nature."

From the sound of it, I have more in common with Calliope than I do with my own mother. I'm comfortable in the darkness. The light makes me nervous.

"Looking back, I'm sure Calliope believed with all her heart that Scott was a god. She feared Clayone would come after him for leverage against Brigit. With all her flaws—and she had many—she was a dedicated mother and loved Scott more than life itself. After Lulu sacrificed her life to protect you, Calliope never recovered. She began to medicate heavily and withdrew from all of us, even Scott. One day, I found a note that she drowned herself in Radley Pond.

"It was your dad's idea to tell you that your mom died of a drug overdose. At the time, we figured it was the best way to keep you away from drugs. Once Calliope drowned herself, we used the car accident story instead of telling Scott the truth. I'm sorry we lied to you about your mother. Drugs tragically belittle the importance of her sacrifice, but of course, everything we've ever done has been to protect you. Now you know the truth, and we can honor her memory. I would prefer to keep the true nature of Calliope's death a secret from Scott. He's a strong, loving boy, but he's not as tough as you."

We continue sitting on the bench, staring at the roses still in bloom though it's mid-September. I put my arm around Gram and turn to look at her. Her eyes are filled with tears.

"Gram, what's wrong?"

"I've lost two daughters to Clayone. I don't want to lose my grandchildren too."

"You won't lose us. I thought Dad said we're protected by the house until Halloween."

"You are protected, but will you be a prisoner at home like I am? Will Scott? I stay here to keep up the enchantments. When I left to check on Ryan at the hospital, Mark and I had to recharge them. And some of the spells will be lifted when you come of age."

"When I'm eighteen?" I ask.

Gram nods. My eighteenth birthday's almost a year and a half away.

I HEARD SCOTT'S ARRIVAL LONG BEFORE HE ROUNDED THE path. First it was the rusty springs of the screen door creaking open and slamming shut. Then it was the pause to pick up Boo Bear who was barking, not to warn us of an intruder, but to beg for a lift. Then it was his hunched shoulders and sad eyes that wanted to plead for forgiveness after a long drawn-out apology.

He possesses an obsessive need to right all his alleged "wrongs," but he has nothing to apologize for. I was the asshole. I was the one who told him his best friend was going to die.

Don't, I think with all my being.

He lifts his head, looking at me like he's confused. He

doesn't fully understand that I'm projecting my thoughts into his mind. He opens his mouth because he's as stubborn as he can be stupid sometimes.

"Don't," I growl. "Don't even think of it."

He pulls in his lips and nods before sitting on the other side of Gram. "So, Gram, you're really a witch, huh?"

She laughs, playfully patting his head. "Honey, do you think most old ladies dress up like witches and cast spells on each other every Halloween?"

His eyes widen. "You and your friends are all witches?"

Over the years, Scott and I have suffered through many of Gram's outrageous Halloween parties and the hordes of friends who came over dressed like witches. If they're all witches, I'd be shocked, and after all the discoveries I've made over the past twenty-four hours, that's significant.

"Well, most of them. The most interesting and exciting ones anyway. Occasionally we invite some non-witches, just for fun, but they tend to be pretty boring and mild mannered. They don't really get into the spirit of the holiday. Of course, for us, it's not called Halloween. It's Samhain. We just use the Christianized name to fit in and not draw any unwanted attention to ourselves."

In addition to Halloween—or Samhain—Gram has bonfire celebrations on other holidays and random nights throughout the year. She builds the huge bonfire behind the greenhouse, hidden from the road. I never thought anything of the location before. I just assumed it was closest to the woods and away from the gardens. I never realized it was to hide from nosy neighbors and prying eyes, especially if they run the Beltane ceremony or other "special" ceremonies. Her friends come from far-off lands just to hang out by the fire—or so I always thought.

"They'll all come this year," she whispers.

"Huh?" Scott and I react as one.

"All the witches, High Priests and Priestesses, Druids, everyone. We'll need their help to cast the spells to keep Clayone away."

"Will it work?" Scott asks.

Never one to hide the truth unless she thought it absolutely necessary, she says, "It has to, or we're all dead."

5

SLEEPING FITS

*S*leep comes in fits. Each time I close my eyes Lizzie's face appears before me, or Ryan's screams fill my ears, or I'm haunted by the terrible laugh that dug its claws right into my back. No matter how many times I toss and turn, sleep refuses to visit me. Finally, in a huff, I shrug off the covers and sneak downstairs. A warm cup of milk might help put me to sleep. Or at least distract me from my brain, which has been a turbulent place these past few nights.

When I turn down the hall, I notice the light's on in the kitchen. For one fearful, exhilarating gasp of a second, I imagine Breas waiting for me. Then I berate myself. I can't stand the bastard, and the whole leaving-town thing was pretty shitty. Dad and Gram have mentioned him a few times, wondering where he wandered off to, as if he got lost on his way home from school or something. If they didn't have so many other things on their minds, they'd probably be more concerned about the missing foreign exchange student, but really who can blame them? No one should be held accountable for hosting that Irish prick. Their lack of concern is forgivable—unlike my romantic notions centering on him. I blame hormones. As much as I try to, sometimes I just can't control them.

If the ding-dong's not in the kitchen, it must be Dad. For as long as I can remember, it's always been Gram and me, with Scott over once a month or so when Dad was out of town. Having them both stay with us now is strange and comforting at the same time. I'm used to having time by myself to think, but maybe I've had too much time to think and shouldn't be alone. My head is a disastrous, treacherous place.

Dad's been pouring through every piece of lore and legend known to man, and as of yet, he hasn't discovered anything he didn't already know.

The answers are known only to women.

And yes, there's that voice in my head—who really needs to learn to shut up. Most people question a person's sanity when they catch her talking to herself, but when a person argues with herself, I'm sure that's cause for commitment.

Towering piles of books are scattered across the table. Dad's hidden behind a large old one. It reminds me of the spell book, but I haven't seen that since it disappeared from the school attic along with Kensey. I creep closer to get a better view of the cover.

He pokes his head out of the book. "Can't sleep, sweetie?"

Thinking back, I probably should have guessed that Uncle Mark was my dad because he's always talked to me in a way I imagine dads talk to their daughters. Sometimes the truth can be right in front of you, but if you're not paying attention, you miss it entirely.

"No," I sigh, grasping the back of one of the oak chairs. I see now that the book he's reading is not the missing spell book. I can't imagine him researching anything possessing dark magic anyway. "Did you find anything?"

"Not yet, but I'll keep searching. I'm hitting an old bookstore and the personal library of a former colleague tomorrow. I'll head out after the funeral," he says, then immediately regrets his words. He's about to tell me he's sorry, and honestly, I can't freaking take another person feeling sorry for me or telling me they're sorry.

"It's okay," I tell him and then feel like kicking my own ass, because I've pretty much just acknowledged that I can read minds, but the cat's out of the bag now. "Lizzie's funeral is tomorrow. No use ignoring it. What if you can't find anything in Pittsburgh?"

I've always been a master at changing the subject. Losing Lizzie is the most difficult thing I've ever had to go through. Talking about her or what's happening tomorrow isn't going to do anybody any good.

"I have a few friends who haven't gotten back to me yet. They're searching as diligently as I am."

"Do they know . . . about me, I mean?" I stumble over the words because I'm not who they think I am, and I don't want to give him any cause to think I believe anything they've told me.

"They know Clayone was released and more or less how. If they aren't familiar with the prophecy, I don't bring it up. The less people who know about you and the prophecy, the better. Believe it or not, there are traitors even in the Celtic world who are willing to sacrifice others to advance their own powers, regardless of the price."

"What if you don't find anything?"

"If we come up empty, I might need to go to Europe. Hit Ireland, Scotland, then England. If necessary, France, Spain, Germany . . . When countries were invaded, monks, priests, and nuns often took books and other works with them when new religious orders forced them into exile. Ireland was constantly at war with itself."

"Can you do that? The semester just started."

"One of the benefits of being a Philosophy professor is that I can say it's research for a paper I'm working on. The head honchos love that stuff."

"Oh . . ." is all I'm able to muster. I hate the idea of my new "dad" leaving Gram, Scott, and me behind.

"Gigi, don't worry. I promise I won't leave you unprotected. Chances are someone will find some information that will help us. Besides, I'm not going to Europe without you."

I'm about to ask him about Scott and Gram, when he raises his hand to interrupt me. "Let's see what we come up with here first before we start making travel plans. All right?" He searches my face for an answer. Times like these it would be useful if he could read minds too. Then I wouldn't have to fully acknowledge my thoughts.

"All right," I reply, but I don't really want to. A comfortable silence settles between us as Dad goes back to his research and I go back to my milk.

I finally realize why I can't sleep. My life might be turned upside down, but Lizzie's life is over.

6

CASKET KNOCKOUTS

unerals bite. The purpose. The pomp and circumstance. The rich leather sofas, the dozen jumbotron flat-screen TVs, and the ornate bathrooms that do everything except wipe your ass. Money made off of dead people horrifies me almost as much as the reason behind the funeral in the first place. Especially this one. I didn't want to come to Lizzie's funeral, but it's the only way I can say goodbye to her. Her parents won't let me into their house, and evidently visiting the morgue is frowned upon. So the only place I can say goodbye to her is at the fancy, over-pimpified funeral home. Selfishly, I want to see her one more time before they dig out a six-foot hole and shove her body into it. I'm relieved that her Jehovah's Witness parents allow "outsiders" to attend the funeral. I guess they aren't worried about non-JWs corrupting the dead. If they knew I killed their daughter, I don't think they'd feel so charitable.

Gram stayed home. I never really thought much about her never leaving our property. It just always seemed that the house, the gardens, and the woods behind us were where she existed. Where she was meant to be. Now, I know different.

That while she loves being there, it is her presence, her being, that keeps the enchantments strong. She wards off evil spirits from entering the property, but even her power isn't enough to keep Clayone away.

"You okay, Gigi?" Dad asks rubbing my arms up and down. Whenever I even think of the Original Werewolf, involuntary shivers grip my body, but it might be the damn air conditioning. They could hang meat in here.

Scott loops his arm through mine. "Follow me, Gi," he says and winds us through the crowd of classmates and their families who are sobbing and hugging one another as if they've just lost their best friend. I want to break their soggy, mascara-covered faces. They act like they knew Lizzie. Like they cared about her. But they weren't her best friend. They didn't kill her.

I did.

I don't care what Dad says, or Gram, or Scott. Especially Scott. I undid the spell. I unleashed Clayone. I killed Lizzie.

"Settle down," Dad whispers as he holds my shoulders. If it weren't for them manhandling me, I'd be smashing my classmates' fucking faces in, and then probably my own.

Why am I here? I shouldn't be here. No one should be here. Funerals should be for old people. Old people who have lived long, full lives. People who have children and grand-children to mourn for them. Funerals should not be for kids like Lizzie. Young. Plucked from their prime. No encore. No happy ending. That coffin shouldn't be her final resting place. It can't be the end of her life.

It should be the end of mine.

Lizzie's mom looks at me, then whispers to her dad. Today will be the first time I've seen them since the hospital. Scott and I went over to their house a few times, but no one was ever home. Or they didn't answer the door even though their cars were in the driveway. I've left messages every hour since the coroner declared Lizzie dead, but no one ever returns my calls. Not that I blame them. I did kill their daughter. I just want to tell them I'm sorry. I want to tell them how much their daughter meant to me. How much she means to me still. Lizzie kept me together. She gave me her friendship when no one else did. She was my person. When she died, the best parts of me died with her, leaving an ugly broken shell.

My eyes keep skimming over the casket. I think I'm relieved it's closed, because even though I want to see her again, I've come to the realization that inside rests the shell of the person I knew as Lizzie. Lizzie—the real Lizzie—the girl full of life and adventure, the girl who'd just found love—is gone. I don't want to see her broken body one more time, but honestly, I'd rather see that than never see her ever again.

Her mom marches up to me. "You shouldn't be here."

"Nancy, she had nothing to do with what happened," Dad whispers to her.

"You and your devil-worshipping ways. When we left the coven, we should have moved far away, so *this thing* wouldn't corrupt her. *This thing* killed her."

Finally, someone is talking sense.

"Nancy, it was just teenagers caught up in mischief," he says in a low even voice as he rests a hand on her shoulder. He's trying to calm her down by touching her, but he doesn't want to release me.

People are beginning to take notice.

"You and this heathen had everything to do with it!" she screams at Dad.

Every eye in the place watches as she stomps away, and then they shift their attention to me, the cause of the commotion. They miss seeing her turn and glare at Dad. They miss seeing her lift her hands and run at him as if he were waving a red cape. They miss her hitting his chest so hard he stumbles back into the casket, and the casket moves. It actually fucking moves. Then smashes to the tile floor.

A thunder clap shatters the shocked silence. The cover falls open.

Everyone gasps—not because Lizzie's dead body smacks the floor, but because the casket is empty. Empty except for shredded fabric and claw marks. Fucking claw marks.

"Noooooooo," Lizzie's mom wails, crashing to the floor beside the empty casket. "Noooooooooooo," she wails over and over.

Lizzie's dad turns to us. "Mark, leave now."

"I truly am sorry, Greg," he says, offering his hand, horrified by what he caused but still trying to salvage some semblance of dignity.

Her dad ignores it, crouching down beside his wife and the empty casket.

My dad stands there, unsure what to do. Unsure where to go. Unsure of everything.

And I come to the realization that I am a disease. I am an epidemic.

My body sinks to the floor in front of the casket. The fucking empty casket that's supposed to carry my Lizzie. I don't want to lose it in front of everyone, but my eyes are stubborn damn things. The floodgates open, and the deluge will drown us all.

"Gigi, come on," Scott pleads, trying to pull my slumped body up. "Let's go sit down."

I refuse to budge, my body completely incapacitated with grief.

A noise escapes my mouth like nothing I've ever heard before. Like nothing anyone has ever heard before.

"Gigi, come on," he says again, but I am unable to move.

Strong arms wrap around me and carry me away from

Lizzie. Well, where Lizzie is supposed to be. But I am beyond caring.

I killed Lizzie.

I killed my mom.

I will kill them all.

7

ABYSMAL HAPPENINGS

*T*he abyss embraces me with open arms. "Welcome," it says. "You'll like it here." My own tomb to bury myself forever.

A light breaks through the wall I've encased myself in and gently squeezes my hand. "Come back to us, Gigi. Come back to us."

Another light kneels in front of me. "I've never seen her like this before," Scott says.

"She lost Lizzie. She loved her," Ryan replies.

Scott rests his hand on Ryan's shoulder. "So did you."

"But Gi loved her in a different way. They were connected by years and friendship."

"Have you been dipping into my dad's Philosophy textbooks when I wasn't looking?" Scott asks.

Ryan laughs. "You really know how to be an ass, don't you?"

"I do try my best."

The weight lifts as my remaining best friends banter back and forth. Eventually I pull myself together enough to become conscious of my surroundings. I'm lying on one of the expensive leather sofas in the sitting room I hate so much. As I'm about to fall into another fit, Ryan squeezes my hand again.

"Ryan?"

"Yeah, it's me. Funny to think that I was worried about making a scene. Compared to you, I'm a heartless bastard," he says with a lighthearted laugh tossed with self-loathing.

It's enough to make me smile.

"Now, that's the Gigi we know and love." He tries to smile too, but the sadness doesn't leave his eyes.

As my reasoning returns, so does my sense of obligation —which I do have by the way. It's just deeply buried most of the time. "You go back in. I'm fine now."

"That's okay. She's not in there."

I sit up. What Ryan says makes sense. "She isn't in there, is she? I mean her body isn't even there."

"Last night she came to me in a dream. She asked me not to come today, but I had to. I knew you'd need me. I knew that even if Lizzie asked you not to come too, you'd come anyway. I came for you."

My eyes tear up. I hadn't slept at all the night before. I refused to close my eyes because I knew Lizzie would visit and ask me not to be here today. But I had to come. I am a selfish bitch.

I stand up and reach for his hand. "What do you think about getting out of here?"

"I'd say, that's the smartest thing anyone's said all day." He absentmindedly fingers the bandages on his neck.

"Stop at the Quikmart for coffee and donuts?"

He stands up with me. "You are a mind full of brilliant ideas today."

If he knew the truth surrounding Lizzie's death, he'd

disagree with me, but he will never discover what happened. I can't lose him too. "You know it."

On our way out, a firm hand slides across my shoulder. "Don't think you're going anywhere without me," Scott says, draping his arms around both of us. The love and goodness exuding from him settles me. With Scott, I can see possibility, even on this afternoon.

If he wasn't in my life, I would be finished.

THE THREE OF US SIP COFFEE ON THE HOOD OF SCOTT'S TRUCK while we watch the ducks floating on Radley Pond. It was Ryan's idea to come here to remember Lizzie. They fell in love down at that dock on those carefree summer days. For him, it's the closest to Lizzie he'll ever get. For me, after discovering the awful truth that Scott's mom drowned herself here, not so much.

"I'm really not looking forward to going back to school," Ryan says, staring out at the water with a wistful expression. A gentle breeze causes little ripples to dance across the pond's surface.

Scott rests his hand on his shoulder. "I don't think any of us are."

"I wish . . . I wish it were me instead of Lizzie," Ryan cries, burying his face in his hands.

I'm sure none of his old girlfriends ever thought they'd see the day that Ryan MacPhee was brought to tears by another girl, but none of them knew the power Lizzie had over him. The power they had over each other. Their relationship, while cut short, was something special. Something lasting. Their love was not something a person can easily forget.

What's left of my heart shatters into pieces.

I wish there was something I could say to make him feel better. To give him some peace. But I can't. I'm worthless.

"But then it would be Lizzie crying over you, and I don't know about you, but Lizzie scared me the most," Scott says.

Ryan lifts his head. I can't tell if he's mad at Scott for finding fault with Lizzie, but I am.

"She wasn't scary," I hiss at them.

Scott hops off the truck. "Really? Did you ever see her when someone talked about you behind your back?"

I jump off after him. "No."

Ryan laughs. "She'd haul off and threaten to tear their eyes out."

Scott holds up his hands. "I wouldn't want to piss her off. I'd take Gigi any day."

"Lizzie? Really?"

"Really," Ryan says. "If anyone dared breath a word of insult against you, she would skin them alive."

I slump against a tree. "Huh. Guess I didn't know everything there was to know about my best friend."

Learning that my best friend was a ferocious protector makes me both sad and proud. There was a side to her I didn't know, a side I didn't know existed. A side she hid from me.

WE ALL NEEDED TIME APART TO WORK THROUGH OUR OWN Lizzie's-not-here shit. Ryan wandered off to the dock. Scott wound up along the shoreline tossing pebbles into the water. As for me, I didn't go as far or feel the need to physically exert myself. Actually, I wanted to do the least amount of exerting possible. I plopped right down on the grass in front of the truck and closed my eyes.

The intense rays of the sun warm me in a way nothing

else can. I just lie still, absorbing the heat, rekindling my soul. A shadow crosses overhead. A whisper of movement dances across my eyelids. I open them to Lizzie, the real Lizzie, with her turquoise hoodie and her secret Twenty One Pilots t-shirt. I sit up, ready to speak, ready to hug her. To never let her go. Maybe even ready to find out what happened at the church. But before I ask her anything, she rests her finger against my lips. I only feel the impression of it rather than her actual touch. She points to Ryan, sleeping on the dock.

Is he okay?

I shrug my shoulders and shake my head "no." There's no point hiding the truth from a dead person.

Will you and Scott take care of him while he's here?

Of course, I mouth to her. We sit staring at each other in silence for a while, until I can't take it anymore. "I miss you."

She smiles at me. "I miss you too, but I really miss kissing that guy. How's Scott?"

"Scott is Scott. He's keeping the rest of us happy just like always. He's my brother, you know."

"That makes sense. I should have seen that. I'm not all-knowing."

"Can anyone else see you? Are you in spirit form? Will you stay like this forever? What happened to your body?"

She holds up her hands. "Whoa, whoa! Obviously my death hasn't curbed your curiosity. I can't give you answers you don't already know, but I guess I'm in an in-between place."

"Like limbo?"

"I guess. I'm not dead, but I'm not alive either. It's like my body is in a deep sleep, but my soul isn't."

"Did someone steal your body? Do you know who?"

"I don't think it was stolen. I think I was summoned."

Dread spawns in my gut. "By who?"

"I don't know, but I'm here now, so let's make the most of it."

"Did you hear that I'm the reincarnated Celtic Goddess Brigit from Scott's story at the campfire? Cause that one's been going around."

"Whoa, what? Have you taken something again? Remember what happened the last time—you were knocked out for the entire weekend. I thought you were going to stop using."

I roll my eyes. "Am I seriously getting lectured from a ghost?"

She pulls her hand to her chest. "We prefer the term 'spirit,' and yes, you are. Someone has to look out for you."

"I can look out for myself, thank you very much."

"Not really."

I swat at her, and my hand sweeps right through her.

"Well, that was weird," she says.

"And awkward. Sorry for trying to hit you."

"Evidently, we spirits don't like violence either. Now, I would mostly love to hang out with you all day, but you seem fine, and Ryan keeps calling for me."

I look over at his still body on the dock. "Looks pretty quiet to me."

"Well, that's why I'm a spirit, and you aren't."

"So, I'm not a reincarnated goddess?"

"I didn't say that, and remember, I can't tell you anything you don't already know."

"Why does this conversation feel very one-sided?"

"Because it is," she winks and disappears, reappearing next to Ryan at the water.

Even though the dock is a good two hundred feet or so away, I focus all my energy on a single thought, *Will I see you again?*

She smiles at me. *I'll always be there when you need me.*

I need you now.

She shakes her head and laughs. *No, you don't, but he does.*

She lies down next to him. He doesn't sit up like I did, but he seems to settle into the dock more and shift toward her.

I smile at them as I shake my head. Nothing like talking to a spirit to uncomplicate your day.

8

NIGHT OF THE WALKING WEREWOLF

*F*or the next week, Ryan is calm. Peaceful even. Scott and I spend every waking moment watching him, studying him, waiting for the first indication that he's turning wolf on us, but nothing comes. No growls. No extra facial hair. No aggression—or no more than he usually demonstrates. We think we're in the clear. We think he escaped the curse. We think wrong.

Hot breath. Hot, stinking breath. And teeth. Sharp teeth ready to bite my jugular. Thoughts that are not my own leap into my subconscious.

The hairs on the back of my neck stand up. I'm instantly aware that someone is in my room. I fight to open my eyes, but my lids are much too heavy with sleep. I shake my head, trying to wake up, feeling that it's a matter of life and death. I kick. I scream. I punch. Finally, I wake up. And I see who's standing in my room, and he's not an invited guest . . .

"Ryan, what are you doing here?"

He doesn't answer he just stares at me with his eyes strangely glowing in the darkness.

"Ryan, what are you doing here?"

The light switches on in my room, temporarily blinding me. When my eyes shift back into focus, I watch Ryan blink once, then blink again. Scott runs in with Dad following behind. Even over the panicked thoughts racing through their minds, I hear the soft shuffle of Gram's slippers on the floor. Her concern is palpable.

Dad grabs hold of Ryan's arm. "What is the meaning of this?"

Ryan gazes at him, bewildered, then back at me. "I don't know," he whispers. "I have no idea how I got here. One minute I'm sleeping in my own bed, and then the next, I'm standing here."

Puzzlement crosses the three of our faces except Dad's and Gram's. In theirs, I see the acknowledgment of an ugly truth.

"Ryan, let me take you downstairs and get you something to drink," Dad says, trying to guide him to the door, but he stays rooted to the spot. "Son? Come on now."

Ryan stiffens. "I am not your son. There is only one that rules me. I will be your slave no longer."

"Ryan, let's go," Scott pleads. He and Dad seize Ryan's arms and drag him out of the room, but it isn't easy. He's gotten stronger. He's probably been hitting the weights to get his mind off Lizzie.

Dad nods at Gram before he shuts the door behind him. She locks it and shoves the key in her pocket. I didn't even know there was a key for the lock. She takes a deep breath. I breathe along with her. I already feel better with her near.

"Gram, what happened? Why did he show up here? Is he upset about Lizzie?"

She sits next to me. "I don't know dear, but Mark and Scott will take care of him," she whispers, stroking my hair.

I notice a bulge in her pocket that's much larger than a key. "What's in there?"

She pats my head. "Nothing you need to worry about. Now, get some sleep, and we'll talk about everything in the morning."

"Tomorrow might be too late. Scott and I need to know the truth. All the truth."

She sighs. "I know, child. Your dad and I learned that lesson the hard way."

Whatever tea blend she gave me earlier puts me right back to sleep, but for the remainder of the night, I sleep in fits, springing up periodically screaming, "What? What?"

Gram tries to reassure me I'm all right each time, but I'm not so sure. There's not much I am sure of anymore. Especially when the warms rays of sunshine wake me, and I expect to feel safe and maybe get some answers, but only discover that the world has become Gigi Brennan's own personal shit show. Entranced by the shiny object lying at my feet, I am completely bewildered. My gaze shifts to Gram's now-empty bathrobe pocket. Still not ready to throw myself out the window and call it a day, I pinch myself to make sure I'm not dreaming, but all it does is assure me that I'm awake. Wide awake. And a shiny silver gun is lying on my bed.

I stare at the woman I thought I knew. The peace-loving, Vietnam-protest-walking, hippie grandmother who doesn't eat meat because it kills animals. And now, she's brought a weapon into my room that kills people. Real-live, honest-to-god people.

I didn't even know she owned a gun. Sure, I carry around a silver bullet good-luck charm, but what is she doing carrying around an instrument of death? I know she believes that I am Brigit, and Clayone wants to kill me, but he is still trapped up in a church, so who is she worried about?

Oh.

My.

God.

"Were you going to shoot Ryan?" I yell.

Her eyes flash open. "What?"

"Were. You. Going. To. Shoot. Ryan?" I enunciate each word so there's no mistaking their meaning. Tears crash down my cheeks.

"Honey, no," she says, shoving the gun back into her pocket. "I just had it as a precaution."

My absolute unraveling has begun. "Precaution? Who are you?" I shriek, shrinking away from her and toward the bedroom door.

She rises from the bed. "Gigi, my job is to protect you."

"Protect me by shooting one of my best friends?" I fumble with the lock on the door, but she has the key.

She sweeps by me to open it. "Gi, child, can we calmly talk about this?"

"There's nothing to talk about!" I storm past her and run down the stairs taking them two at a time and almost slam into Dad.

"Gi, what's wrong?"

"What's wrong? What's wrong? My own flesh and blood was going to kill one of my best friends. That's what's wrong!" I rush past him, in no mood for his lessons. I stomp to the back door and push on it, only to discover that it's locked too. The forces of the universe are working against me, and I think I might explode. "Since when did we start locking doors anyway?" I growl as I struggle to open it.

"Since my best friend snuck into my sister's room," Scott whispers with a sadness that will overwhelm me if I let it.

"Scott, what's wrong?"

"What's wrong is that my best friend tried to kill you!" Dark circles rim his green eyes.

I cross my arms. "He didn't try to kill me."

"What was he doing in your room then?"

"He was probably thinking about Lizzie and sleepwalked over out of habit. I'm the closest thing to her he has left."

"You're also the closest thing to a goddess the world has ever known."

"Don't tell me you believe that crap. I thought we decided the prophecy was a bunch of garbage."

He stares at me. "But what if it's not? What if you are Brigit? Ryan was here to kill you, Gigi. He's turning into a werewolf. I know it. You know it. You saw how he acted last night. We can't ignore it any longer."

"So, what does that mean? We have to kill one of our best friends? I already killed one. I don't want to kill another one."

Dad walks in with Gram at his side. Dark circles ring their eyes. The last few weeks have aged them. They've aged us too. "You won't have to."

"You are not killing Ryan."

"Gi, child, we might not have a choice," Gram says. "There's a much bigger picture here. We have a responsibility to protect you, my granddaughter, but we also have an even greater responsibility to protect the Goddess Brigit."

"We are not discussing that again."

She steps toward me. I try to back out of the room, but with the door locked, I've nowhere to go.

"It's time you start accepting responsibility for your actions. It's not just your life. It's all our lives. It's life as we know it. If Clayone wins by killing you, the world will be plunged into a place of endless horror. Werewolves capable of killing at will. You must believe you are Brigit. You must accept who you are."

I'm about to argue with her when she clutches her chest and collapses, and suddenly, nothing else matters.

9

TWISTING THE KNIFE

*D*ad hasn't let me stay at the hospital with Gram since she's been there. Each night he checks the doors and windows in the house, then locks my bedroom door, and he and Scott sleep on my cold, hard bedroom floor. I argue with him. Complain about privacy and not needing their protection. But quietly, inwardly, without Gram around, I find their presence reassuring. She wasn't as healthy as we all thought she was. She had a heart attack.

Tonight's the full moon. Not the Super Blue Blood Moon—that's not until Samhain at the end of the month. This one is October's first full moon, a seemingly benign one, far away from the thirty-first. But evidently, all full moons generate power that can be harvested. As a result, my normal imprisonment routine will come after Dad's special little ceremony tonight. With Gram's absence, the spells and enchantments once cast on the house and the property have lost some potency—or that's what he told me. He's invited all the covens and their members to add their own magic to our house in preparation for the next one, which happens to be on Halloween, which also happens to be Samhain, which also happens to be the day Clayone will try to kill me because he thinks I'm the Goddess Brigit reincarnated.

Yeah, they still believe that shit.

If I could, I'd run away and make everyone's life a lot less complicated, but I won't leave Gram. I just want this night to be over.

Throughout the evening, a steady processional of believers walk into our kitchen and bid me thanks for my sacrifice of immortality to join their lives. Their reverence for me makes me want to vomit and become violent. Dad, Gram, and Scott warned me to remain polite, so instead of disagreeing with them, I bite my lip. Instead of punching them, I dig my nails into my palms so hard they bleed.

There's probably a giant neon red arrow flashing above my head that says "Fraud Alert," but I continue along with my B-movie script. I nod my head, graciously accepting their appreciation, but since I don't acknowledge them with words my throat doesn't light on fire. I just wish they could see me for what I really am—a stupid, selfish sixteen-year-old girl who doesn't have a clue who she is or where she's supposed to go.

The conversation I had with Gram at the hospital earlier makes me feel even more like a fraud. Worse. A liar. A terrible liar. And I've always prided myself on trying to tell her the truth. Granted, it hasn't always worked out that way, but I made an attempt. I lie to other people, but not to Gram.

"Gigi, you must accept who you are," she said. "You must acknowledge the truth and embrace it to realize your full power."

"I do!"

"No, you don't. I know you well enough to know when you're lying. Besides, I can read your mind too—did you forget that?"

Actually, I kinda did. I tried to block my brain from her, and when I couldn't, I tried to think goddess-y thoughts.

"Gigi, you have to Believe you are Brigit. Belief gives power. Without Belief you are nothing."

I nodded along with her, thinking, okay, okay, I believe. I believe.

"Don't you dare act condescending to me, missy."

Gram had never scolded me or been so angry with me. Her words put me in a place that made me scared I might lose her, and I can't lose Gram. I can't.

"Missy? Is that anyway to speak to a goddess?"

"It is when she's your granddaughter. You need to protect yourself. Don't worry about Scott or Mark or me or anyone else. You must protect yourself at all costs."

"I understand."

She jumped up in bed, setting the machines off in a frenzy of beeping. I wanted to tell her to settle down, but she was on a rant, and not even the Goddess herself could stop her. "Do you? Do you really understand? What I'm saying, Gigi, is that you will not be able to make everyone better. In the end, you will need to make some hard choices. Choices that revolve around life and death. If you are killed, life as we know it will be over. It won't matter how many lives you saved. It won't matter how many people or animals you helped. Clayone will rule the Earth and destroy at will. He cannot be granted that power. Protect yourself."

"Yes, Gram."

"You must Believe who you are," she kept saying, over and over again, even after the nurses came in and made her lie back down. Even after they shooed me out after I kissed her good night. Her words, the belief she had in her words, will be forever etched in my brain.

Another patron of Brigit shuffles into the kitchen. I know exactly what his intentions are—if only I could admit I can read minds without acknowledging I'm a goddess, my life would be a lot easier. And maybe I'd have less of a desire to hit people, because I wouldn't need to hear their homage speeches twice.

I massage my temples in hopes that maybe he'll get the hint.

"Ah, I understand. Goddess work must be very taxing," a voice says with a haughty touch of sarcasm in his Irish lilt.

I glance up at the visitor, delighted with the lack of reverence in his voice. He's old. Really old. Like maybe older than Gram. He reminds me more of Gandalf than Dumbledore. His long white beard is tied neatly in the middle, and it nearly touches the floor. His shoulders round in on themselves from a lifetime of experience, but he holds his head high. His face reminds me of the bark of a pine tree, but his eyes sparkle with more life and knowledge than anyone I've ever met.

"Have I met your approval?" he asks.

"Quite," I tease, feeling more lighthearted than I have in days.

He reaches out his hand. "Good. It's a pleasure to meet you, Gigi."

The palm of his hand reminds me of a soft, warm hug.

"A pleasure to meet you, Amorin. Dad told us all about you."

Amorin was Dad's mentor in Ireland. He lived with him while studying Druidry and the craft for many years until he fell in love with Calliope and moved to Vernal Falls. That's when the complications began.

Speaking of which, Scott walks in with Dad.

"Well, I'll be hog-tired and ticked 'til the cows come home," Amorin says with a fake southern accent as he shifts his attention to Scott. "Mark, you didn't mention we're not just protecting a goddess, we're protecting a god as well."

Dad steps backward. "Excuse me?"

"The prophecy of course . . .

One of love, one of light,
Spring forth from the womb
To guard from the night.

The power to heal. The power of youth.
Their existence to all a living proof.

As immortality weighs,
One shall fall, one shall rise,
To perish from all humankind."

"Amorin, I'm well aware of the prophecy. I'm just not sure what you mean."

"Mark, don't you see? Both of your children are part of the prophecy. 'One of light . . . The power to heal,' refers to Oegden, Brigit's brother. Your son has a powerful aura around him, but I suspect it's invisible to you because of your relationship."

Dad gapes at Scott like he's never set eyes on him before, while Scott and I stare wide-eyed at each other. His question to me is obvious. *What the hell is going on?*

I shrug my shoulders in answer, thrilled the topic of discussion is not about me for a change. He winces at my smirk before turning his attention back to Dad and Amorin.

Finally, Dad gasps, "I can't believe I didn't see it. Calliope always proclaimed she had a vision she'd give birth to a god, but no one believed her. We dismissed her vision so easily, while wholly embracing Lulu's. Scott does embody Oegden —his love and affection, his charisma, his charms, his mischievous nature. I can't believe I didn't realize it sooner . . ."

Scott squirms around in his chair, the undivided attention making him uncomfortable.

Good. Now he knows how I feel.

Abruptly, Dad declares with grim determination, "No one else can know this. If Clayone discovers he can destroy a goddess and a god, he will stop at nothing to do so. If he can destroy them, he very well might be able to take control of this world with no interference from the other gods."

"Okay, first, I don't believe for one iota that I am the Goddess Brigit, but wouldn't the other gods fight if two of their kind are threatened or killed?"

"I wish it were that simple," Dad says. "The gods are disgusted with our treatment of Earth and her creatures. My trips to the Otherworld have confirmed this. They might just let Clayone take control of Earth and remain forever in the Otherworld where they can stay fat and lazy," he says with venom rivaling my own. I didn't know he possessed such fire.

"They wouldn't protect their own kind?"

Amorin rests a hand on Mark's shoulder, instantly calming him. "Mark, would you mind if I explain it to the children?"

"Be my guest. I need to go outside and prepare for the ceremony. Gigi, Scott, lock the door as soon as Amorin leaves, and do not open it for anyone. Do not leave the house for any reason. If the entrance or exit opens during the ceremony, the spells we cast tonight will be broken. Do you understand?"

We nod our heads obediently. He hugs and kisses us before leaving.

"Now, where was I . . . ?" Amorin says and then pauses to scratch his chin for an exorbitant amount of time.

Scott and I glance at each other out of the corner of our eyes. We don't want to be rude, but Amorin is really old. Maybe he's forgotten we're even here. I'm about to clear my throat when suddenly he begins his tale.

"For several millennia, the gods have watched over and guided their creations with love and attention, but like a human, a god's interest can wane from time to time. He might be tired of all his hard work going unnoticed. She might be offended that she's no longer worshipped in the manner she used to be. He might enjoy lying around getting fat and lazy as your father suggested, or jealousy could play a role. Gods are notoriously envious of each other, especially if one is held in higher esteem by our world than another. Following the birth of Jesus Christ, a great influx of Christianity spread throughout Europe. Many pagan religions, including Druidry, changed dramatically.

"Christian missionaries managed to extinguish many of the Celtic gods while absorbing others into their religion. There was no real method to the madness. Early on, it had to do with convenience . . . Certain areas of Ireland fervently believed in and followed Brigit, and so, the practical monks and bishops of the time turned Brigit into one of their saints, whereby ensuring Brigit's power across the ages. On the same token, many other gods and goddesses were not honored or remembered. As a result, their power greatly diminished, and their jealousy grew.

"If Brigit, one of the most powerful Celtic goddesses, is destroyed, her powers will be distributed among the remaining gods. What the gods don't realize is that if Brigit's life is taken, they will all become vulnerable. Clayone crossed into the Otherworld once before to try to kill her. She managed to expel him, but he has proven extremely resourceful and will try to find a way back in if the opportunity presents itself. He patiently waits for the chance to destroy Brigit while human.

"During one of her earlier reincarnations, the first settlers of Ireland, the Tuatha De' Danann, nearly destroyed one another as they fought over land and power. The day of Brigit's birth, a flame rose to the heavens signaling to the world she had arrived. She hoped to inspire people to unite together and believe in her rather than kill one another. As her fame grew, peace spread throughout the land, but during a full moon on Samhain, a dark witch reopened a passage from the Otherworld releasing several Fomorians. The Tuatha De' Danann joined her in an epic battle against Fomorians, werewolves, and dark witches, but they were greatly outnumbered. As the warriors lay wounded and dying across the land, Brigit used the last of her mortal magical power to create a lake to cure their injuries, and with her Vessel of Life she could bring the dead back to life. During her weakened state, Clayone seized the opportunity to try and kill her, but she managed to escape back into the Otherworld through a secret entrance moments before obliteration."

The possibility of bringing Lizzie back to life certainly sparks my interest. I straighten up in my chair. "The Vessel of Life . . . What is that?"

"Brigit possessed a cauldron that she used to bring the dead back to life, but she could only use it in times of great need and mass extermination. When used singularly, the spirit splits in half, because nothing can be given that isn't taken away. Returning to life comes with a great cost."

"Where would one find this Vessel of Life?"

"That, my dear, is the great mystery. On the day of the

battle Brigit presented herself with the Vessel, but there is no record of her bringing a single life back from dead—for there would be legends and tales heralding her as a savior of her people. The belief is that the Vessel of Life disappeared for all of time. No one knows what happened to it."

Just my freaking luck. The one thing that could bring Lizzie back from the dead, and it's been missing for a few thousand years.

Gigi, Lizzie is gone. Let her rest in peace.

I will never find peace until I find the Vessel of Life. Lizzie lost her life because of me. The least I could do is give it back to her.

"You might ask yourself, Why would Brigit risk destruction at each mortal reincarnation?"

No, I actually wasn't thinking that at all, but if Brigit did reincarnate, maybe I can ask her where she hid her Vessel of Life.

"It is vital for her to feel the lifeblood of humans. Their emotions spill over into their every action and reaction. Nothing in the Otherworld rivals the emotions felt on this plane. While she doesn't often give up her immortality, she does so in times of great need. Times when our world needs her more than the Otherworld."

Scott leans forward in his seat. "Amorin, you and Dad keep referring to the Otherworld. What is it? Is it a place anyone can visit?"

"Scott, I'm glad you asked. A good habit I might add. Never be afraid to ask questions. Never be afraid to question the answers. Never take anything for granted," he says, holding his hands together with his pointy fingers aimed at us. "The Otherworld is a paradise where souls go to find respite until they are ready to reincarnate back into this world. A place for gods and goddesses to live in pleasure and relaxation, as opposed to the Underworld, which is reserved for traitors, sorcerers, and evil beings. When a soul enters the Underworld, they do not come back. In the Otherworld, old age, sickness, and death do not exist. Happiness lasts forever, and time has no meaning, no beginning, no end. Unfortunately, it is also home to dangerous forces that thrive on power and destruction, such as the Fomorians who are unable to return back to this world unassisted but seek entrance nonetheless.

"In the modern era, many of the entrances to the Otherworld have been destroyed. The remaining entryways are scattered throughout the world, generally forgotten. Ireland still has a few, but each portal possesses its own form of entrance. Often times a heavy mist falls upon a person seeking answers. The person soon finds himself in the Otherworld, a beautiful place, tempting him every step of his journey to remain there forever. The visitor must not stay long, or he forfeits his time in this world.

"Most often followers conduct ceremonies like we will tonight and visit the Otherworld in spirit form. This evening we will communicate with some of the inhabitants and perhaps discover answers, but it is up to us to decipher the meaning."

His eyes twinkle with the memory of his many visits to the Otherworld, both in spirit and otherwise. I try to gauge exactly how old Amorin is, but like Gandalf, he is ageless, and I think maybe he will live forever.

SWAN LOVE

"Now, let me tell you about Oegden. The story of Oegden is one of the most romantic love stories you will ever hear. Oegden, like many young gods, roamed between the worlds, breaking hearts everywhere he went."

Scott, a well-known lady killer, gives me a smug grin. He feels justified that he's never settled down with one girl.

"One night, Oegden dreamt of a woman more beautiful than any he had ever laid eyes on—her intellect brilliant, her tongue sharp, and her will stubborn. When he woke in the morning, he knew he had to have her. He and his brother set out to search for her. They searched for one year but still could not find her. With each passing day Oegden's love grew stronger, and he became more and more desperate. No other woman would satisfy him.

"One day, rumors of an enchanted princess reached Oegden's brother. He went to the lake where the princess allegedly lived, but the tribe's people refused to talk. He stayed two nights trying to find news of the princess. On his third and final night, he stood at the water's edge contemplating what he would tell his brother, what lie he could spin, when a lovely white swan swam to shore. Before his very eyes, the swan transformed into a breathtaking young woman. He knew he had found his brother's mate.

"For three weeks, he begged the woman to come with him and meet his brother, but she refused. Instead she requested Oegden come to her and live as a swan for seven years. If he remained true to her during that time, she would consider marrying him. The next day, the brother left to share the news with Oegden, doubtful his brother would concede to the princess's proposal.

"Without hesitation, without even seeing the princess in earthly form, Oegden changed into a swan and flew to the lake where his love lived. The princess was coy in nature and made Oegden search for her among the huge flocks that lived on the lake, but the search didn't take long. The moment he laid eyes on her, he knew who she was. For seven years he courted her on the water, and they fell in love. They were often seen with their necks intertwined in an embrace creating what we now call a heart—the universal sign of love."

I glance over at Scott, pretending to gag, but his eyes are glazed over with a dreamy expression on his face.

"Oegden was not absorbed into Christianity. Sadly, he's rarely even discussed in Celtic mythology, but as the God of Youth and Love, he strives to remember what it's like to fall in love when you're young. Every young love reinforces his power. The passion and emotion of love is what entices him to reincarnate as a human from time to time.

"He and Brigit are as devoted as I suspect you two are. If Clayone is truly as close to threatening Brigit's reign as we presume he is, Oegden is here to protect her. According to the prophecy, the two of you can defeat Clayone if you work together. The problem is you only have a month to learn the spells and incantations that other followers have studied for decades and still haven't perfected. And although we'll lay heavy protections on this house tonight and on Samhain, we may not be able to keep Clayone out. If I'm being entirely forthright with you, the odds are presently not in our favor. But then, I've never been a gambling man."

He stands up and places his hands on our heads. "It is time for me to attend the bonfire. I bid you both farewell for now."

Scott locks the door behind him. Solemnness seeps into the room. Not that Amorin persuaded me that I am Brigit, but he absolutely convinced me Scott is Oegden. A constant source of strength and support for me, Scott possesses extraordinary gifts of love and understanding. I am absolutely dedicated to my purpose this evening—protecting Scott at all costs.

He begins setting out candles at various locations around the perimeter of the oak table. I follow him clockwise as he casts a ceremonial circle by pointing his finger at the ground. From what Dad told us, the circle is meant to keep unexpected visitors from the Otherworld confined within the circle. He starts with an incantation Dad taught us.

"From the ground to the sky, I cast this circle. I conjure a sacred place between our worlds. The circle is cast."

Turning to the east, Scott lights the yellow candle. *"Spirit of the East, element of Air, I ask you guard us from sudden storms and protect us with gentle breezes."*

Then he turns to the red candle representing the south. He lights it as he says, *"Spirt of the South, element of Fire, I ask you guard us from raging fires and warm us with controlled flames."*

From the south, he turns to the green candle. *"Spirit of the West, element of Earth, I ask you guard us from disturbance by providing firm footing."*

I peek over at him as he turns to light the final blue

candle representing the north. From his expression, I know he believes every word.

"Spirit of the North, element of Water, I ask you guard us from tidal waves and cradle us in calm waters as gentle as a mother's arms."

I mouth the incantation with Scott, but I lack his sincerity. When the incantation is complete, he sits in silence, eyes closed, breathing deeply. From what I've heard, meditation can be a useful tool, but for me, it's too abstract. I feel like I should be doing something—visiting Gram, researching legends to help Ryan, anything besides sitting here. I peek over at Scott. His face is completely relaxed as he whispers quietly to himself. Finally, his earnestness inspires me to make an attempt at meditation. As I focus on my breath, I try to clear my mind of random scattered thoughts. After a few moments of intense concentration, a tingling sensation develops in my fingertips and toes. My mind begins to drift off to another place. A lush green place. The richness of color makes me want to cry. It doesn't seem possible that such beauty exists.

A harsh ringing breaks the silence—ugly and disjointed in this wonderful place. Abruptly, my spirit violently pulls back and plops me into the hard wooden chair. Scott and I stare blankly at each other, unable to speak. Suddenly, the phone rings again. An overwhelming sense of foreboding consumes me as Scott reaches for it.

"Hello?" he asks tentatively, trying to ground himself back into this world.

As he listens, his face turns white. He drops the phone and takes one look at me before rushing outside to Dad.

There's no need to verbalize what I already know.

Gram's dead.

11
SHIT SHOW

*U*nable to move or think, I stare out the kitchen window. The moon looms large before me—beautiful and full. The wind picks up. Beating against the window. Ripping dry leaves off the trees. Blowing dark clouds in to hide the moon's existence.

The back door bursts open. Nails scratch across the floor like nails on a chalkboard. Heavy breathing fills the space.

Before me stands a hideous creature. Half-man, half-wolf. Long mangy fur with sharp canines salivating in anticipation of its next meal, green eyes sadly familiar to me, and a mind intent on death.

"Ryan," I say in a low voice, conscious that the slightest movement might set him off.

"I am here to avenge my master's imprisonment and set all my kind free," growls the creature.

"You are Ryan. You love Lizzie. Scott and I are your best friends." I'm not ready to let the beast take full possession of my friend.

"You lie," he snarls. His rotting breath wafts across the room. "You are my enemy. I must kill you."

I remain motionless, painfully aware that my life is in this creature's hands. My heart pounds a drum roll in my chest as a reminder of my own mortality.

Abruptly, the creature springs onto the table with teeth bared, transforming into an even more terrifying monster. I leap out of my chair and throw it at him, then sprint down the hallway to the stairs, hoping to lock myself in my room before he gets there.

A blood-curdling howl shatters the silence as the wolf leaps from the table.

Taking the stairs two by two, I strive to get away. Hot breath on the back of my neck tells me it's only a matter of seconds before the beast tears me apart and everyone will finally realize that I am not Brigit, that I am nothing more than a foolish girl who mistakenly released a terrible monster and killed one of her best friends in the process. I propel myself forward as fast as I can go, but it's not fast enough. Sharp claws swipe at my sides, trying to pull me back down the stairs. Blood seeps from the wounds, but instead of distracting the beast, it spurs him to move faster. Hot rancid breath burns my ears, and I know the end is coming soon. He will not stop until his bloodlust is sated.

His teeth clamp down on my hood, knocking me down onto the remaining steps before he descends upon me.

"Ryan, no!" I shout, clawing and kicking at him, but he's too strong. Whatever once remained of my friend has disappeared. He throws back his head in a victorious celebration before his teeth prepare to clamp down on my throat.

The end nears . . .

And I welcome it.

. . .

A SHOT SHATTERS THE SPACE BETWEEN US. AT THE BEAST'S hesitation, I roll out of the way. He lands next to me, filling the span of stairs with his body.

I lie beside him, trying to catch my breath, until I realize the steady rise and ebb of the heartbeat next to me is waning. A compelling need to help any injured creature overrides my sense of reason. The fur covering Ryan's face recedes, and there, lying before me, is my dear friend. I lift his hand and smile down at him. "Hey."

"I'm sorry," he mouths to me.

"Is it still alive?"

I peek over my shoulder to see Scott standing at the foot of the stairs with a gun in his hand. Wisps of smoke spiral out of the shaft.

"Ryan is, but not for long," I whisper. "You can come up. It's okay."

When he sees Ryan's fully revealed face, he sits down on the other side of him and takes hold of his hand.

Ryan smiles weakly at him, but his life force is leaving him quickly. As it drains from his body, I become aware of someone else on the stairs with us.

"He's almost with me," Lizzie whispers. Her excitement seeps into the world of the living, but I don't share it. There is no victory in death. I hand Ryan's hand to her.

Scott watches the arm dangling in midair and jumps up. "Is that . . . is that who I think it is?"

Lizzie winks at me.

"She came for Ryan."

I lean down and kiss him on his forehead, which is still warm but won't be for long. His face grows peaceful, and his body relaxes into the stairs. His spirit form rises from the lifeless body, no longer constrained by gravity.

"Goodbye, Gigi, and thank you," his spirit says. Then he

gives Scott a giant bear hug. Tears stream down Scott's face as he returns it.

Lizzie touches my shoulder. "You have a long journey before you, but soon we will meet."

"I thought you weren't supposed to tell me anything I didn't already know."

She smiles at me. "I didn't."

Lizzie and Ryan descend the stairs. Dad, Amorin, and many of the coven members have congregated at the base of the stairs. Although there is a dead body in front of me and a dark pool of blood dripping down the steps, they possess expressions of sheer wonder as they observe us. I don't know if they can see Lizzie and Ryan, but just as the spirits are about to pass directly through them, they step aside.

As Lizzie and Ryan disappear through the front door, my attention returns to the lifeless form on the stairs. Scott sinks down onto the steps beside Ryan's body. He can't believe he killed his best friend.

And that's when reality hits . . . What will become of Scott?

Lawyer buzzwords fly around in my brain.

Brutal murder. Absolutely.

In cold blood. What could be more terrible than shooting your best friend in the back?

Premediated. Got that right. Silver bullets aren't easy to come by.

Unprovoked. Could probably argue that one, but who would believe us? There's no evidence to prove our friend had become a werewolf. No evidence to even suggest he, in fact, was after me. Ready to kill me. The only proof of evil intention is the dead body on the floor and the smoking gun in Scott's hand.

Verdict: Guilty. That's what the lawyers will call it. That's what the jury will decide. And who can argue otherwise? The gun was in his hand. His best friend dead on the stairs beside him. They'll call him a monster. Lock him away.

My only consolation is that he will be protected behind strong steel bars. His prison cell will allow him to sleep without fear of retribution.

I, on the other hand, may never sleep again, afraid the second I close my eyes my worst nightmare will come lurking on the other side of my pitifully weak wooden door.

12

LIES AND DECEPTIONS

I didn't agree with what they planned. I fought. I yelled, but they acted as they always do. Like I don't have a say in the future. Like I don't know what's best for me—which I know is true. But the thing is, I know what's best for Scott, and their brilliant plan isn't it.

Dad stands in front of his son with his phone in his hand. "Are you ready?"

Scott nods then takes a double shot of whiskey. Jameson Irish Whiskey. The same type Breas and I drank, which led to yet another hookup. Some are addicted to pills. Some are addicted to illegal substances. I was addicted to Breas, until he broke the habit by leaving.

I watch with growing apprehension as Dad dials 911. When the operator asks him what his emergency is, he says, "There's been a terrible accident. Someone's been shot. Send emergency services and the police right away." After the operator confirms his address, he ends the call and pours Scott another double.

Most of the coven members have left. Amorin and two other women remain to bear witness.

All too soon, bright red and blue lights flood the living room as the ambulance and police cars pull in.

"Scott, you don't have to do this," I whisper.

"Yes, I do," he says before taking another shot. "You're my sister. I will protect you."

My fist slams into the wall. Why must everyone in my family be so stubborn? When do I get to take care of them? What am I going to do without Scott?

Dad opens the door. The paramedics rush in with a stretcher. I step away from Ryan and let them attempt to resuscitate him. I know their efforts will be wasted, but it always makes people feel better if they know they've done everything they can to save someone.

"Hello, Officer Smith, Officer Lamberton," Dad says.

"Why is it I've been to your residence more in one month than I've been to any other house in Vernal Falls in the past ten years?" Office Smith scratches his head.

"I've asked myself that same question."

Officer Lamberton watches the paramedics work on Ryan. Finally, they shake their head. One of them says, "I'm calling it . . ."

Officer Smith sighs and takes out his notepad. "What happened?"

Scott stands up, sways back and forth, and collapses back into the sofa. He doesn't need to act drunk. He is drunk. "Ryan and I were sneaking shots of whiskey in the kitchen when everyone else was outside at the bonfi-re. I told Ryan about this cool old gun Gram owns, and he wanted to see it. So, I showed him!"

"Then what happened?" Officer Lamberton asks.

"Whelp, we started playing a-round with it. Cops and robbers, and Ryan was the robber, so I chased him up the stairs. Then I tripped and shot him," he whispers, sobbing to himself. No amount of alcohol can remove that sting.

Officer Smith shoves the notebook back into his front shirt pocket. "We've got to take him down to the station, Mark."

"I know," Dad says. "I'd like him locked up in one of those juvie programs."

"Isn't that a bit harsh?" Officer Lamberton asks.

"I'm afraid I wasn't strict enough. Ryan paid for it with his life, and his parents will suffer from my lack of parenting."

Officer Smith hands Officer Lamberton the handcuffs. "You have the right to remain silent . . ." he begins, and I fall into a blubbery mess. Amorin wraps his arms around me. Through swollen eyes, I watch as Scott is taken away in handcuffs, and Ryan leaves on a stretcher with a white sheet pulled over him.

When will I get to save the ones I love?

13

LIFE SUCKS

*A*ll alone, I stare out the kitchen window. The full moon shines in the cloudless sky. The brightness spills into the room, a bitter reminder of its power and the terrible toll it exacted on my family. A lifetime of memories flash before me . . .

My first ice cream sundae with Scott; my second-grade birthday party with Scott, Lizzie, and me in a pink princess dress with a matching party hat; sharing secrets with Lizzie, with Scott always close by; Gram kissing me good night; Gram knowing when I needed a hug; Gram, Gram, Gram . . . and the day Calliope betrayed us all. Instead of feeling joy or pain or anger, I feel nothing at all. I am too numb to feel ever again.

Soft moccasins shuffle across the kitchen floor, sounding empty and lifeless. Dad flops down in a chair across from me, finally allowing the weight of the day to catch up with him. I pretend to be mesmerized by the knot on the table that has fascinated me as far back as I can remember.

"How did Ryan get in here? I thought there were spells protecting the house."

Dad releases a heavy sigh. "I don't know. Maybe were-wolves are like vampires . . . once he's welcomed in, he can come and go as he pleases. Or maybe the oak thresholds and doors don't hold the same power over him because he's been here so many times. Or since the back door was opened while we were putting new enchantments on, all the previous defenses were broken. We will never know how he got in."

I bite my lip, realizing the man with all the answers has none to give.

"Gigi, do you want to talk about what happened?"

I don't know if he means Gram, Ryan, Scott, Lizzie, Clay-one, or the whole goddess nonsense, but the answer is "No," on all accounts.

"In the morning, I need to go to the police station and the hospital to fill out some paperwork. Amorin will be around to keep you company. I just booked three seats on a flight to Ireland. We fly out at 4:00 p.m. tomorrow afternoon."

"Tomorrow? What about Gram's funeral? What about Ryan's? What about Scott?"

He folds my hand into his. "Gigi, there's no time left. We have less than thirty days to figure out how to protect you. We can't risk staying in this house. The spells and enchantments are gone. You would be provided with no protection whatsoever."

"But how do you know? You don't know for sure."

He sighs. "The truth is, much of the magic placed on the house remained in place because Gram lived here. She chose to never leave the property in order to ensure your protection. Think of it like a mist or a veil over the house and you. Now that she's gone, the veil has lifted."

I jerk my hand away from him. "I don't care about my protection. I care about Gram, Scott, and Ryan."

His eyes tear up. "I know you do, but Scott will be

protected. The juvenile detention program lasts seven weeks. As for Gram and Ryan, there's nothing more we can do here for them. Honor them by accepting your position."

I swipe at an errant tear. I will not be guilted into pretending to be a goddess in order to clear his conscience or anyone else's.

As I open my mouth, he raises his hand. "Regardless of what you believe, our best chance of honoring your grandmother and mother's memory, to honor Lizzie and Ryan's memory, to honor Scott, is to take every precaution necessary and protect you. Kildare, Ireland, is a long way off from Vernal Falls, Pennsylvania. Amorin lives in a small hamlet near Saint Brigit's Cathedral. There isn't a place on earth safer."

I'm about to argue, but he shakes his head. "I don't want to fight with you. I haven't the strength left."

And that's when I realize that I'm not the only one who has lost someone.

JOURNEYS TO OTHER PLACES

The thought of entering the kitchen without Gram makes me sick. I thought a world without Lizzie in it was torturous enough, but with Ryan and Gram gone too, the end must be near. Without thinking about it, without intending to, I find myself at the ritual area behind the greenhouse. Amorin pokes at the remnants of the charred wood from the fire the night before.

"I don't know why I'm here," I whisper.

He raises a white, wiry eyebrow. "Don't you?"

"I want to visit the Otherworld."

"And so, we shall." He tosses some bundles of dried herbs into the hot ashes. As if by magic, the flames spring back to life, devouring the herbs. Sage, sandalwood, frankincense, and rosemary release into the air and mix with the comforting smell of wood smoke. A sense of calmness settles over me as I prepare the ritual circle. Instead of reciting the incantation Dad taught me, I chant words that come to me as natural as breathing.

To cast this circle from Earth to Fire, from Water to Air, join together with Spirit to guide me to the answers I seek. I give you my love, my light, to show me the path to truth.

To the East, I give to you my love, my light, to show me the path to truth.

To the South, I give to you my love, my light, to show me the path to truth.

To the West, I give to you my love, my light, to show me the path to truth.

To the North, I give to you my love, my light, to show me the path to truth.

As I light the final candle casting the circle, electricity begins to surge through me. Breathing deeply, I focus my thoughts toward finding a way to protect Scott and rid the world of Clayone. A tingling sensation reaches down to my fingers and my toes as I'm transported to the place I visited while meditating with Scott the evening before. Instead of being abruptly jettisoned back to reality, I observe a place more beautiful than I can fathom, greener than anywhere I've ever been. Energy pulses around me as I observe the lush landscape. Emerald-green hills sprawl farther than my sight can reach. Sparkling blue-green streams form breathtaking waterfalls that cascade onto rocks glowing with a translucent quality to them. Magnificent flying creatures challenge my imagination into believing that maybe unicorns, fairies, and dragons really do exist. Without purposely taking a step, I move closer to the fairies flitting about on a large green bush. I float over the ground, no longer constrained by my human form. A freedom I've never felt before rises within me as I glide across the landscape surveying this magical place, the Otherworld.

Brilliant rays of sunlight shine down from the heavens onto an enormous oak tree spanning several stories, it's branches like fingers reaching out and touching the sky. I sweep across the field toward the tree and find a cobblestone path meandering down the steep slope.

From above, I can see a rose garden in the distance, and I know that's my destination. A complicated hedge maze of vibrant holly blocks my path. In the real world, corn mazes were the bane of my existence, but I don't feel the least bit intimidated. Confidence grows within me where normally self-doubt takes root. Upon entering the labyrinth, I take a right without hesitation. At each intersection I turn left or right without thinking about it. After dozens of turns, I enter the beautiful courtyard filled with roses. There's a familiar worn garden bench off to the east side of the courtyard. I hurry over, hoping Gram will be there, but find only a dusty old book lying in the spot she normally sits. In disappointment, I pick it up. It reminds me of the old spell book I found in Gram's attic, but this time I can read the title: *Briguathe Grimoire*. I look up and realize I'm back home with Amorin sitting opposite me.

"Where was I?"

His eyes twinkle with mischief. "Where do you think you were?"

"I don't know. A place I've never been before."

"Are you sure?"

"No . . . I'm not. There was a maze, a complicated maze that blocked my path, and somehow, I got through it. Like I knew which direction to head. Does that make sense?"

"It makes perfect sense. Did you see anyone?"

"No. I was hoping I'd see Gram. I did find an old book."

He leans in. "Oh?"

"The title was *Briguathe Grimoire*. Do you know it?"

He pulls at his beard thoughtfully. There is nothing I can do to speed up his response. He answers in his own due time, which pushes the boundaries of my patience. But I wait and wait, and hope, and . . .

My god, I hope he freaking answers soon!

And finally, after I've cycled through various types of torture that would get him to talk, he answers my question.

"I am not familiar with the tome, but it possesses the information you need."

Shit. Way to pop my fucking high. What the hell am I going to do now?

"Not to worry, Gigi, there are hundreds of annals that the monks and nuns wrote at Saint Brigit's Cathedral in Kildare. I'm one of the curators of the Cathedral Library. I've no doubt your book is within its confines. Between the three of us, we'll find it." He stands up and puts his arm out for me. "Now, you must finish packing for your long journey."

Amorin's like the grandfather I never had. The one I never knew I needed. I find solace in his company. A gentle guide, not replacing Gram, but the other arm of her. He seems wise for the most part, but there's one question that I have to ask him.

"Why do you believe I'm Brigit?"

He turns to me, gently taking my hands in his. His clear blue eyes search mine. "Why don't you?"

To that, I have no answer.

15

BUMPY FLIGHT

*T*he Vessel's within reach. Well, except for the hulking body of Clayone, half-man, half-wolf, standing in front of it. Blood pours out of Scott. He doesn't have much time left. I need to get Clayone away from him before it's too late.

Tears stream down my face as I consider my next move. Running into the meadow will lure Clayone away, but Scott might die in the meantime. If I fight him here, will there be enough time to retrieve the Vessel and save Scott before Clayone destroys me?

"Gigi, you must protect yourself at all costs. It doesn't matter how many lives you save if Clayone wins in the end. Protect yourself," Gram chants. "Protect yourself."

"I can't. I can't leave him. I can't! I can't!" I scream. Desperation rakes through me. "Don't make me choose. Don't make me choose."

"Gigi, wake up, honey. You're dreaming. Honey, wake up!" Dad gently nudges me. "It's getting worse," he murmurs to Amorin as I rub my eyes. I can't escape the feeling of dread that Scott's in mortal danger and I'm stuck in an airplane between Dad and Amorin instead of protecting him.

"We must wait until she's ready," Amorin whispers back.

I try to read their minds, but they've blocked themselves to me. Spell work probably, or Druid rune protection, or a combination of the two. But I haven't the strength to break through. Scott lying on the ground in a pool of blood is all I can picture along with the line from the prophecy, "One will fall."

From the airport, a train takes us to Amorin's village. Along the way, a countryside of endless green pastures with little sign of civilization rolls past my window. Amorin's home is a half hour's walk to Saint Brigit's Cathedral in Kildare, but Dad insists we wait until morning to visit the library.

"Welcome to my home. You'll find what it lacks in size, it makes up for in character," he says, leading us down the path.

From the thatched roof to the wooden shutters to the stone foundation, his cottage is exactly what I envisioned it to be, with the exception of the two broomsticks hanging above the front door.

"Your transportation?"

"Believe it or not, they are supposed to keep evil witches from entering the house. They must work, because I haven't found one inside yet," he says, winking at me.

It's all too easy to fall into a smile with Amorin around, but I don't want to smile. I want to cry. I want to rip down the baskets from his ceiling, because they remind me of Gram's place. I want to toss the drying herbs into the fire and leave, because it feels so much like home it makes me hurt. Because Gram isn't in it, and she never will be.

Dad picks up a book from the stack on an end table. "Trying to learn something new, Amorin?" He flips the cover for me to see, *Journey to the Otherworld*.

Amorin sets a kettle of water on the stovetop. "I saw it and couldn't resist. For thousands of years, followers studied under an experienced Druid for a decade or more. Now anyone can buy a book on Druidry at a local bookstore and study the craft. It blimey blows my mind. Where would I be without my mentor? Where would you be?"

"Times have changed, and we need to change with it or go extinct. The true practitioners will put in the time. At least now, more people can read about the craft and decide for themselves whether they want to become more involved or not. These books educate people that we aren't flying around on broomsticks and casting hexes on our enemies. We're peace-loving, Earth-centered followers. It's time the damage wrought by Caesar, Shakespeare, and Hollywood is vanquished. Once people learn the truth, our cause will grow," Dad says, leafing through the book.

"You've always been a progressive thinker, Mark. I hope you're right on this one, and small covens of Dark Arts followers don't spring up all over the world. But enough talk about troublesome affairs for the evening. Let's have some tea and biscuits before retiring."

He carries over a tray with a bright blue- and green-wash teapot that reminds me of Gram. He pours the tea into a matching cup and offers it to me, Gram's pottery stamp in plain view. The mug almost slips out of my hand at the shock of having a part of Gram with me in Ireland. I want her with me always. At least I have a piece of her here.

As I bring the tea to my lips, my sense of smell alerts me that Amorin slipped a sleeping potion into it. Thoughts of sneaking out immediately enter my mind. I pretend to drink it as Dad and Amorin make small talk about the weather. I may not be able to read their minds, but I know they're trying to lull me into sleep. After a few minutes I yawn and stretch. The required performance takes little effort. While they're engrossed in conversation, I dump the tea into the sink. As I wish them good night, I yawn again for good measure.

A short while later my bedroom door creaks open. I lie still with my eyes closed, breathing in and out, hoping Dad will buy my act. I've been through this scene a hundred times with Gram. Eventually he closes the door, but it takes a ridiculously long time. He's far less trusting than Gram was, or else he knows me better than I realize. I wait until two sets of snores drill through the thin walls of the cottage before I slip out the window and into the night.

16

CREEPY CATHEDRALS

Racing across the countryside, a heightened sense of possibility rushes through me. Tonight I will find that book. I will finally get to protect the ones I love. I will fix this mess before anyone else I love dies as a consequence of my stupidity.

In the distance the white turrets of Saint Brigit's Cathedral stick out above the ancient trees. One soars higher than the rest. One holds the treasure I seek.

A soft light glows from a side entrance. The hairs on the back of my neck shoot up. A sinister shape emerges from the shadow just to the side of the entrance, morphing into an old woman wearing a black robe and carrying a lantern.

"May I help you, dear?"

There's nothing about the old woman's appearance that suggests danger, but something about her unsettles me. And I can't read her mind, which is both frustrating and a relief.

"I know it's late, but . . ."

"Late? It's not late. It's just the right time," she says.

I immediately warm to her.

"Could I come in? I just got here, and I've been dying to

see the Cathedral my entire life. I've taken the Google Earth walking tour about a thousand times. There's this book I've wanted to read . . ."

She opens the door for me. "Books we have, but we have thousands." She leads me down a long hall and through a large archway. She stops and lifts her lantern, illuminating a room over two stories tall, covered from floor to ceiling with books. "Can you be more specific?"

I step away from her and toward the nearest shelf. It's easier to lie to someone when you're not face to face, or sleeve to robe in this case. "Actually, no. I dreamt about a book that was really old, and I wanted to see if I could find it." I realize far too late that I've revealed too much. My mind reading's been off since arriving in Ireland, and so, evidently, is my ability to lie well.

She studies me. My neck prickles from fear. Terror. I don't know, but it's enough to make me want to run away and hide. Fortunately, my desire to find the book overrides my irrational fear.

"Well, that is another story," she says. "Books we dream about have extremely powerful magic tied to them."

I choke on my spit. "Magic?" I cough. "Isn't this cathedral a Christian memorial?"

She shakes her head as she laughs. "It is, dear, but magic can be found everywhere. For instance, Saint Brigit is said to control the harvest and bring the dead back into the world of the living. How is that not magic?"

I nod to humor her and also to hide my shock, because I'm freaking floored right now. "Do you have any books on Saint Brigit?"

She puts some books on the closest shelf. "Oh, there are many books on Saint Brigit written by mundane Catholics much too imbedded in this world to even consider the possibility of an Otherworld."

I step toward her. "Otherworld. You've been there?" Then I remember to play it cool. "I mean, Otherworld, what's that?"

"Dear, you don't have to pretend with me. You can trust old Carman. I knew you belonged to the Order of Brigit the moment you stepped into the candlelight. Each follower of Brigit has an aura a seer won't miss. I myself have been a follower all my life."

She takes my hands into her ice-cold ones. I think it's to reassure me, but it fills me with something else.

Dread I think.

17

PILES OF SOMETHING

*G*ram never got the chance to share anything with me about the Order of Brigit, with the exception of a few details. I'm sure she assumed, like I did, that we'd have years together. Decades maybe. But now she's gone, and her life story's gone with her. As a member of the Order, Carman seems to be the closest thing to Gram I have left.

"You're still in her service?" I stare at Carman with a newfound respect. "I thought most followers left the Order when their thirty years were up." Gram never mentioned any choice to remain in her service forever.

Carman pulls at a black onyx crystal necklace. It could be my imagination, but the stone shifts and swirls when she touches it as if it's alive and trying to speak. Or get out.

"I chose to stay. I love working here with Her books, Her works, Her spirit. There is no place I would rather be. I've waited all my life for a moment to be in Her presence, and I will remain until she returns."

I wander over to the other side of the room and pull a

random book about winemaking from the shelf. "I hope your wish comes true."

"Oh, I'm sure it will. The moment is close at hand. Very close indeed. Now, let me show you some books you might be interested in."

She gestures for me to follow her. I reluctantly put back the winemaking book, which might be useful in the future. All those grapevines outside Amorin's cottage ought to serve some purpose other than making a complicated and painful escape route. The library magically expands with each step, reminding me of Hermione's purse. Surely a dream come true for booklovers and Potter fans alike. I'm impressed that Dad was able to restrain himself from visiting until morning.

Carman winds her way through the shelves, pulling books as she goes. She eventually places them on a table deep within the catacombs of the Cathedral. "Sit, and I'll bring you more."

In a way, Carman reminds me of Gram. Powerful, commanding of respect, and old, in addition to her being a member of the Order. I suppose that's why I listened to her and sat down instead of searching for the one book I needed to find. A book that isn't in the pile.

Without Gram to guide me, maybe Carman will help me find my path. Not replace her—no one could replace Gram— but maybe fill the void. Maybe help guide someone who needs serious guidance.

She hefts a mighty pile onto the table. "Here are some more for you, dear."

"I would have helped you carry them."

She waves me off. "I've got strong arms from decades of carrying around books, but the bones are tired. I'll retire to my room if you don't need me anymore this evening."

"I'm fine, Carman, and thank you."

"No, thank you. I love meeting new followers. Leave the

books on the table. I'll put them away in the morning. Good night, dear," she says, shuffling away.

"Good night, Carman," I call after her, but she's already gone, disappearing back into the shelves from whence she came. And yes, I used "whence." Ancient library equates to appropriate ancient verbiage.

Henceforth, I shall continue to use such language until such time that I grow bored or decide to commit a particularly heinous act. I laugh to myself, having entirely too much fun. I decide to quit yammering and get to work. None of the books from the three towering piles even resembles the one from my vision, but rather than ignore the hard work Carman went through to gather them for me, I decide to indulge her efforts for the time being. I've got a soft spot for old people.

The spine cracks as I open the first one from the largest pile. A gorgeous, hand-painted picture covers the first two pages along with the caption, "As Earth meets Sky, so too will Dagda and Anu join and create divine children who shall be celebrated for the ages."

Intrigued, I continue reading.

DAGDA AND ANU, MOTHER EARTH AND FATHER SKY, called many different names but nearly universal across every faith and religion, were prolific in their childbearing, but none of their children were as celebrated or beloved as their third daughter, the Goddess of Healing and Fertility, Inspiration and Poetry, Divination and Prophecy, Fire and the Forge, known simply as Brigit.

AND SHUT.

The only "chosen" daughter I want to read about is Queen

of the Damned.

After wasting hours searching the shelves, scouring the spines of hundreds, probably thousands of books, and finding nothing, I return to the table ready to cause some destruction. Without any gasoline to torch the place, Carman's piles might be my best bet. At the top of one of them, there's an old leather journal that I missed earlier. The only hint of a title is the shadow of gold left in some of the letter grooves. The leather, the binding, and the pages are similar to the spell book I found in Gram's attic.

Someone scrawled spells and incantations along the margins in this one too. The spell work fascinates me, but the rhythm of them seems different, reminding me more of the curses in the other spell book, but not exactly. A folded piece of parchment slips out from between the pages. Upon opening it, I realize I just found my very own Marauder's Map. Well, not people moving around in a there's-Severus-Snape-walking-the-halls-mischief-managed kind of way, but seven features are clearly identified with runes written around them. A rectangular-shaped block tower with what looks like a small castle sits on top of a hill in the center of the map. The Cathedral is clearly marked with an intricate cross just north of the castle, and an enormous tree grows between the Cathedral and the castle. In the northeast corner of the map there's a round block tower with one lonely window, and to the west is a large mound. I passed the grassy mound on my way to the Cathedral. It must be more than just a pile of dirt and rocks. I'll check that out on my way back. Amorin's hamlet isn't on the map, whether because it's too far west or too small I can't say. At the southeastern section there's a huge bonfire with figures dressed in fur dancing around it. The people are drawn with such detail it's almost like they'll step off the page. A woman at the center with her arms raised in the air commands the dancers. At the very edge, there's a hamlet, or at least a square building with a cluster of smaller buildings. I wonder who lives there.

Of course, the thought of stealing the map crosses my mind. I mean, who would know? There's no one in the library except Carman and me, and she went off to bed, so really it's just me. Herein lies the conflict. The brainwashing Scott and I received as children leads me to question my own map-thievery actions. We weren't subjected to anything as aggressive as shock therapy or waterboarding, but we were taught that books were to be treated with respect. Defacing a cover or marking an interior page was akin to committing one of the deadly sins—although I guess since we're not Christians, that falls into a gray area.

Perhaps if I copy it . . .

I take a piece of paper from the sketchbook in my backpack and make a few attempts at tracing it before scrapping the entire operation. It's too damn dark in here to make tower from mounds of the features. I glance around to make sure no one's watching as I fold the map along the creases and shove it into my back pocket along with my pathetic attempt at forgery.

Adrenaline pulses through me at the theft. I haven't felt a rush like this in a very long time, but it's pulling at my conscience. I rub my hands up and down my legs, trying to convince myself that no harm was caused to the book. Someone probably filed the map in the book by accident or put it inside for safekeeping, and now, it's safely stowed in my pocket. End of story.

No book was damaged in the making of this robbery.

I take another deep breath and flip to the next page, where I almost shit myself. A wolf creature leaps out ready to snap my neck.

Well, I guess it didn't actually leap off the page, but it certainly looked like it did. With its long mangy hair and powerful canine teeth capable of ripping a person's throat out in one bite. And eyes, though different from Ryan's, still sadly human.

"Populations of werewolves exist all over the world, but they all can be traced back to Clayone, the Original Werewolf."

Merely reading his name, sends shivers down my spine. An eerie feeling of being watched settles over me. I reach into my pocket and withdraw the pepper spray I managed to smuggle past airport security. Cautiously, I turn around, searching the dark entryway of the library for the source of my discomfort. Even though I don't see anyone, that doesn't mean someone's not there. I've been through enough to know that things hide in the shadows—as in my guardian stalker from Vernal Falls, though fortunately/unfortunately he's a few thousand miles away. I call out, "Hel-loo?" hating that I sound like a freaking chicken. It'll destroy my reputation.

When no one answers, I return to my work.

INVULNERABILITY, AGGRESSION, AND SUPERHUMAN STRENGTH and speed are typical werewolf traits that carry over to human form. Highly loyal to their pack and leader, they can prove to be invaluable allies. Curses can be placed on werewolves when in human form to force obedience to a "master," similar to a household dog.

THE AUTHOR VIEWS WEREWOLVES AS TOOLS TO BE USED AND manipulated. No one should be forced to carry out another's purpose. And while I'm well aware that the Original Werewolf wants to kill me, no one deserves to live under subjugation. Free will makes us human.

WEREWOLVES CAN BE CREATED IN A VARIETY OF WAYS. THE most common and well-known method of transformation comes from the bite of another werewolf. This type of werewolf is the most vulnerable to death by the silver bullet or silver dagger, but it's will is the easiest to control.

THE NIGHT RYAN FIRST CAME TO MY ROOM, HE DIDN'T KNOW what he was doing there. He was surprised to find himself in my room. But his words that night will forever be etched in my brain: *"I am not your son. There is only one that rules me. I will be your slave no longer."* That wasn't Ryan speaking. Did Clayone manipulate him into attacking me? Gram and Mark were under the impression that Clayone's weakness kept him locked in that church until the full moon, which was the night Ryan attacked. So wouldn't he have been too weak to manipulate Ryan that first night? And Ryan couldn't have found his way back up to the church. He would have said something to me or Scott. So then who was the "only one" Ryan was talking about?

As I return to the picture, the eyes of the wolf no longer fill me with terror. Clayone might want to kill me, but this wolf is human. Ryan was human.

ONLY INDIVIDUALS WITH A STRONG BACKGROUND IN witchcraft should attempt the second method of transformation. On the night of a full moon on either a solstice or a Sabbat, tie an individual to a marble alter. Slice his wrists to rid him of most of his blood. Inject a vial of werewolf blood into his veins. The timing is crucial. If the victim retains too much of his own blood, the change may not occur. If the victim loses too much blood, he may die, unless injected with large quantities of werewolf blood. When this happens, death may still be the result. Decide if the victim is worth the quantity of werewolf blood needed to save his life. The younger the participant, the more obedient the werewolf will be to its creator.

THE GRUESOME GUIDE TO WEREWOLF CREATION IS ABSOLUTELY fascinating.

BEWARE THAT WEREWOLVES WITH INJECTED BLOOD, ESPECIALLY those with large quantities, can be highly volatile and participate in extremely self-destructive behaviors. They tend to be difficult to control, but their heightened aggression and strength often make up for their poor self-restraint.

I TURN BACK TO THE BEGINNING OF THE BOOK IN SEARCH OF A title page, but none exists. Morbid curiosity and a glutton for punishment keep me reading. My own strain of shock therapy.

THE THIRD TYPE OF WEREWOLF IS THE MOST OBEDIENT. IT IS extremely powerful, nearly impossible to kill, and the most difficult to create. Planning, preparation, and timing are key elements to success. The full moon, on either a solstice or Sabbat, is ideal for intercourse when the werewolf is in wolf form. A willing female participant who is a witch is preferred but not fundamental to success. Spellbinding and hypnosis are two common methods of persuasion if the female participant is reluctant. Hypnosis has the additional effect of keeping the female in a coma-like state for the duration of the pregnancy, which lasts for nine months. The birthing process always results in death.

BECOMING INCREASINGLY UNEASY WITH THE CONTENTS OF THE book, I glance through the scrawled notes in the margin.

Restraint of the werewolf during creation must be used to ensure the life of the consort.

The more powerful the werewolf, the more powerful the offspring.

Werewolves often form packs with an alpha male as their leader, similar to wolves in the natural world. Occasionally, lower order members vie for power. The alpha must dominate the aggressor through a demonstration of strength. If the aggressor does not submit to the alpha, death is normally the outcome for either the assailant or the leader.

Werewolves possess voracious sexual appetites. On the night of a full moon, they are known to take multiple partners. Three to four nights preceding the full moon, their sexual arousal increases dramatically. During this time, most werewolves are incapable of curbing their sexual appetite.

What began as a "How-To Guide for Werewolf Creation" has turned into "Facts about Sex with Werewolves," which I suppose if I wanted to have sex with a werewolf would be useful, but since the Original one wants to kill me, learning insider tricks is not especially helpful. Unless of course it reveals some way I can stay alive, which would be awesome. Mostly it's downright disturbing, and coming from me, that should say something.

18

DISCOVERIES AND STRANGERS

"Gigi, there you are!" Dad rushes over to me. "We've been searching everywhere for you."

My head feels like I spent the night at a rave. "Huh?"

"We've been searching everywhere for you. We suspected you would come to the library, but it doesn't open until 8:00 a.m."

My eyes feel like the sandman had his way with them. "No, it's open all night. Carman showed me around. She's a follower of Brigit."

"Gigi, there's no one named Carman who works here. I personally know all the employees."

"Maybe she was hired when you were gone. All I know is that there's a woman named Carman who showed me around last night. Here, look at the stack of books she brought me."

He studies the pile. "Dear, why would she give you these books to read?"

"I don't know. I told her I dreamt about a book, and she

said books we dream about are very powerful. She gave me these, then went to bed. What's the big deal?"

"Most of these books deal with the Dark Arts of Witchcraft. Any dedicated follower stays far away from these books. Is this all of them?" He watches me, ready to discover the truth even if it means studying my body language for the hint of a lie.

After a cursory glance, I nod my head. As his attention shifts back to the books, I nonchalantly look around my seat. The largest volume—the one with the map and the werewolf how-to—is gone, but I'm not going to draw attention to its disappearance or open myself up to the Amorin/Dad inquisition about the book.

Amorin lifts a stack. "Did you find the book you were looking for?"

His eyes seem hungry to me. Immediately my guard goes back up.

"I didn't. How old is this cathedral?"

"It was built around 1223 AD for defense as well as worship. The original castle was built around 450 AD. Only the foundation, a few walls, and the tower remain. The rest was destroyed."

That must be the castle on the map.

"Through the centuries, Kildare fell victim to numerous invasions and shifts of power. Most of the town has been rebuilt numerous times. Eventually the invaders, namely the Catholics, realized how dedicated the Celts were to Brigit. In an attempt to convert as many pagan Celts as possible to Christianity, Brigit was brought into the church as a Saint," he says, but instead of reverence to Brigit I note a bitterness in his gentle voice.

In the shadows of a hallway, Carman watches us. I'm not sure why, but I decide to keep that information to myself.

"Can you take me to the original ruins?"

. . .

THE FRESH MORNING AIR OF IRELAND FILLS ME WITH ENERGY. It normally takes me two or three espressos made from the dregs of the carafe at the Quikmart to feel so awake. As we walk across the grass, the largest tree I've ever seen sprawls across the field. It's long-reaching branches touch the earth, the sky, and the horizon. Several scraps of paper fly into my hand. All I need to do is make a fist to catch them.

"What is that tree?" I ask in wonder.

Dad rests his hand on my shoulder. "That, dear Gigi, is Brigit's Tree. Pagans and Christian's alike flock to the tree every year and ask for Brigit's favor in blessing them."

I open the worn notes I caught.

"Dearest Brigit, please honor me with a baby. I promise to be a loving and caring mother. Love, Amy."

"Brigit, Goddess of Fertility, please bless my child now and always with your love and protection. Dedicated to you always, Jen."

Amorin rests his warm hands beneath mine as I cradle the wishes. "Brigit is the Goddess of Fertility of Land, Animals, and People. Women pray to her for assistance in pregnancy and childbirth or for the blessing of fertility."

"So I've heard," I whisper. A new yoke of pressure forms on my shoulders. Any more and my neck will snap.

Suddenly, a warm breeze envelops me. The scent of lavender and lemongrass pervade it. A small purple butterfly dances on the breeze. Leaving my troubles behind, I skip across the field after it. The ground bounces with my every step, inviting me to join in on the fun, but all too soon, hard, unforgiving stone replaces the softness, and I find myself in what must be the ruins. Tall, lichen-covered, tumbledown stone walls surround me. A fleeting sense of déjà vu leaves me with the irresistible urge to pull up a particular carved flat brown stone in the floor, but it's something I must do by myself.

"Is there something you remember?" Dad asks, hunching over to catch his breath. Amorin trails in a few seconds later.

"No, nothing. I was trying to catch the butterfly."

Sadness fills his eyes, but I don't want to give him false hope. I am not Brigit. There are merely things I know.

Heavy footsteps stomp behind me. Amorin's and Dad's eyes round. For a fleeting moment, I'm terrified it's Clayone, but then I realize it's the middle of the day, and we're in the new moon phase. Turning cautiously, I find myself face to face with a large hairy brown cow. I stumble backward in shock. The cow follows me, getting close enough that I can see air steam out of its nostrils. Close enough that its long pink tongue sticks out and licks my face.

"Ewww, gross!"

The only reply I receive is, "Mooooooo," before getting another sloppy sandpaper kiss from a second cow who appears before me.

Dad and Amorin have a right jolly chuckle.

"Gigi, Brigit had two pet cows that followed her everywhere during her time at Kildare. Through the many years of turmoil and assault on the Cathedral, descendants of the cows have remained."

I nod my head, acknowledging Amorin's words but remain silent. For once, I'm glad Scott's not around. He'd have a field day. Pet cows—seriously?

19

LOVE BITES FOR REALS

*L*ife in Ireland bites. Or, to be more clear, *my* life in Ireland bites. Pouring over musty old books that make me sneeze (because I'm allergic to either ancient knowledge or antique mold) makes for a real drag on life.

The countdown to the Super Blue Blood Moon lunar eclipse approaches, and we aren't any closer to figuring out how to stop Clayone than we were a month ago. Honestly, at this point, without Gram, Lizzie, and Ryan—even without Scott—I'm ready for Clayone to have his way with me and be done with it. Which I know is crazy talk, but if I don't find some action soon, I'll go insane. Certifiably insane.

My only fun revolves around hanging out at the mound on that map, which is some raised lump of dirt too uniform to be a natural land formation but too far removed from any signs of civilization to be man-made. Unless, of course, it's a freak of nature, which would explain why I like it so much.

But today it bores me too. I mean, I'm ready to give in and die at the hands of the Original Werewolf, so logically my afternoon reflection times aren't enlightening me to a greater purpose other than becoming doggie kibble. By four o'clock, I'm ready to torch the place. As thoughts of gasoline and matches swirl around my head, I leave the mound behind and wander the green hills of the countryside in search of something, anything, to entertain my mind. Somewhere along the way, the path shifts from worn grass to cobblestones. The cottages, once spread out and infrequent, begin to butt up next to each other. In the far-off distance, the faint hum of music draws me to it, the moth to the flame. I wind through streets, wandering deeper into Kildare. As the music grows louder, I move faster. I need to escape for a little while.

I need to escape forever.

My backpack is on the dresser back at Amorin's, but I'm not worried. I know how to get what I want, and what I want is to get into the club. My leather jacket provides automatic sex appeal, but that, too, is hanging in the closet at Amorin's. Since coming to Ireland, my mind's been too preoccupied to think about going out on the town. But here, now, I'm ready for action. I unzip my hoodie to reveal the cleavage. It doesn't always work for free drinks, but it always works to get into the club. The bouncer gives me the once-over before tilting his head at the red door. Someone scrawled "Welcome to the Devil's Den" on a chalkboard, and I know I've come to the right place.

The outside looks like all the other storefronts—brick walls, awning, and one large window—but the inside opens up into an endless cavern of badass music and kick-ass dancing. Immediately, I throw my arms out and thrash to the music. It's like coming home, and I know I've found my place. And this time I don't need to catch a ride with a stranger, steal someone's car for the evening, or get a driver. I can walk here.

As I surrender to the music, a nameless partner moves with me. Tall. Dark. Beautiful.

Our bodies don't touch, but there's no space between us. The outline of his face is barely visible in the darkness. But I feel like I've known him before. I feel like I've known him forever. Song after song we remain together.

Heat.

Movement.

No end.

No beginning.

He's all I want. He's all I need.

We fall into a familiar rhythm.

The heat, skin temperature. I remember it all.

Sweet escape.

Sweet nothingness.

20

GREEN EYES AND SCONES

*M*y pounding head reminds me of last night's foray. I quietly groan as I bring my hand to my head, hoping, for once, I've been blessed with a healing touch. After a few minutes I realize I've no such luck. In fact, now it feels like ice picks are stabbing into my brain. All the coven believes I am Brigit, Goddess of Healing, but here I am causing damage to myself. I groan again, pulling the covers over my head, returning back to a wonderful cocoon state.

"Rough night last night?" laughs an unfamiliar male voice with a thick Irish accent.

I sit up, searching for the source, but the curtains are drawn, and there's nothing but darkness and shadow. "Who are you? Where am I?"

"You don't remember me? We seemed to get along quite well last night," he laughs again. A white crooked smile flashes out at me as he leans forward in the chair next to the bed.

I don't know whether to be scared or rip his clothes off.

"I don't understand. How did I get here? Why don't I remember anything? Oh god, did I? Did we?" I stumble on my words as I try to remember what went on at the club and afterwards. I peek under the covers to make sure I still have my clothes on. Which I do. Which is a relief.

"You are an inquisitive one, aren't you? Adventurous and inquisitive. I like that in a girl." He leans closer, searching my face for an answer before he even asks the question, "Would it be so bad if we did?"

I involuntarily shiver under his intense green eyes that almost glow in the darkness. I try to answer him, but my brain turns to a useless pile of shit.

"Well, would it?" he presses, leaning closer still, his eyes locked on mine, and I wonder if he's going to kiss me, because I certainly wouldn't mind if he did. Then suddenly, somehow, I manage to sever the spell, and I remember how to breathe, and I certainly remember my words and how to use them.

"Yes! I don't even know you. I don't even know your name. I'm not even from Ireland." Not that any of those reasons have stopped me before, but somehow it seems like a smart argument, and the truth is that even though I've had past hookups with people I don't know, I have never, never, *never*, spent the night at their house, and that's what freaks me out the most. I have never been in this situation before. I try leaping out of bed, but my legs get tangled in the sheets, and I fall into his chest.

"If you wanted me in bed with you, all you had to do was ask," he teases, cradling me to him. I breathe in his heady scent. Everything about him is familiar to me. He sets me back down on the bed, and I already miss his touch.

"Have we met before?" I search his face for answers, but he only smiles as he sits down beside me and offers me his hand. "We're meeting now. I'm Alaric."

"This feels like an awfully formal introduction after spending the night together. I'm Gigi."

"Did you have something else in mind?" he says, looping his arm around my shoulders.

My heart races, and I realize that maybe I shouldn't have poked the beast. He'd overpower me in less than a second.

"Just relax and take a deep breath," he says.

When I don't follow his advice, he shifts me gently away from him, so we can see each other's faces.

"I promise I will never hurt you. Do you believe me?"

Spellbound, I manage to nod along with him.

"Good," he says, resting me back against his chest. "It's not every day a siofra comes into my life."

"Shee-fra? What's that?"

"A Celtic fairy. You are exactly what I envision a fairy to look like."

I relax into his embrace, finding comfort and peace with a complete and utter stranger.

After a few minutes, he shifts away from me. "Better?"

"Better."

"Now," he says, reaching for my hand, "let's get you some breakfast. You're but a wee little thing."

I allow him to pull me to him, before stiffening my arm. "Seriously, you are going to start cracking short jokes."

"I would never joke about my fairy queen, especially after all we've done." He raises an eyebrow suggestively.

"We did have sex, didn't we." I don't know why that would mortify me, but it does to my very core. My cheeks glow with embarrassment—also new to me.

He lets me sweat it out for far too long, before he grins. "We didn't. I was a gentleman. You, on the other hand, were a complete banshee."

I punch in the arm. "Oh, shut it. I was not."

He rubs the spot. "For a wee little thing, you pack a punch. Now, what would my siofra like for breakfast?"

"You keep calling me your siofra. Isn't that a bit presumptuous?" Although I'm actually kinda thrilled at his term of endearment for me.

"Did you not dance with me all night?"

"Yes, but . . ."

"Did you not stay here last night?"

"Yes, but . . ."

"Are you not crazy about me?"

"Yes, but . . . Hey, you tricked me!" He catches my hand as I swat at him—as if he already knew what I was thinking.

"You were merely answering my questions honestly."

I'm about to protest, but he places his finger across my lips. His confidence greatly underscores my desire to argue, and I realize I've hooked up with dozens of guys and girls, but I've never interacted with them after our physical exchange. My boots were on, and I was out the door before they could ask for my number or if they could see me again. Even with Breas, we never actually talked. With Alaric, everything is different. I want it to be different.

"Now, let's get my siofra some breakfast, and then I'll take you home."

Home. Shit. Dad and Amorin must be going out of their minds. "I really should go . . ."

"I'll take you after you eat. No arguments," he says, leading me down the hall into a kitchen remarkably similar to Amorin's. He ushers me over to a round oak table and pulls out a chair for me.

"Help yourself," he says, sitting down next to me.

Someone—Was it Alaric?—set out a pitcher of orange juice, a pile of scones, and a bowl of fresh fruit.

"Were you expecting company, or do you always have company?" I pick up a blueberry scone, trying not to sound possessive or interested, but I am definitely both.

"I wish I could take credit. My nan laid out breakfast for

us. And, no, I don't always have company. Normally, I stay at the girl's place."

The scone crumbles in my hand.

He hands me a new scone, then brushes a lock of my white hair behind my ear, leaving a length of black hanging down in front. "Kidding. Sometimes Nan just knows when good things are coming around the corner. Eat! You need your strength."

He adds some fruit to my plate and pours me some orange juice before getting his own breakfast ready. With his attention placed on the scone, I consider his features. His green eyes have almost a supernatural glow to them, even in the low light of the kitchen. His black hair, gently tousled from sleep, makes me want to run my fingers through it. His jaw is strong and well defined, and he has the most kissable lips I've ever laid eyes on. In all definitions of gorgeous, he's it.

"Have I satisfied your appraisal?" he asks as he swallows his bite.

I reach for the orange juice. "Excuse me? I don't know what you're talking about."

He turns the full power of his gaze on me. "Were you or were you not checking me out?"

I tear apart my scone. "I wasn't checking you out."

"I studied you last night while you slept. I figure you should have a few minutes to do the same. Do you like what you see? And be honest."

I refuse to meet his eyes and fall under his enchantment again, but I decide to answer honestly—also new. "As a matter of fact, I do."

"Likewise," he says, mirroring my self-righteous act, which makes me giggle. Actually giggle. Me, Gigi Brennan, giggling. What the hell's wrong with me? But giggling feels good. Great actually. I haven't felt this light since . . . Lizzie died. I shudder at my realization.

"Is everything all right, Gi?"

Surprise. Pain. Anger. I latch onto these emotions. "Why did you call me that? How do you know my nickname?"

He raises his palms to me. "You told me."

I throw down my napkin and stand up. "I didn't."

He rushes over to block my exit. "Gigi, calm down. You told me your name last night right before you fell asleep. You're not a very trusting person, are you?"

I step away from him. "I have my reasons."

He folds me into a powerful embrace that dissipates all the hurt that once rushed through me. "I never want to let you go," he whispers, breathing me in.

I breathe him in too, and think to myself, I don't want you to either.

21

MYTH BUSTERS

*A*laric dropped me off at Amorin's cottage gate, leaving me with a sweet kiss on my forehead to last me until our next encounter, which cannot come fast enough.

"Until we meet again, and I hope it's soon," he whispered, then lifted his foot back on the footrest of his motorcycle and sped off down the country road.

I watched him until he disappeared around the bend then sighed. I have never felt so content, so at peace with my world. With Alaric everything feels different, and that should scare me, but for some reason, I welcome it.

The front door swings open, and Amorin rushes down the path with dark circles under his eyes.

"Gigi, dear, where have you been?"

Guilt rakes through me. I thought only about myself last night. I forgot that Dad and Amorin would worry about me. Or I didn't care. I didn't care about anyone but myself and my own desires.

Selfish bitch, step right up.

"Amorin, I'm sorry. I went to a club and wound up staying

at a friend's house." A very sexy friend. "I wasn't thinking. I was stupid. It won't happen again."

"Gigi," he says, "you are a sixteen-year-old girl who has had a tremendous burden placed upon her. You are allowed to be stupid sometimes. You are allowed to act on your impulses. It's the reason why you're here."

My eyes fill in response. His belief in me is overwhelming and misplaced.

"Where's Dad?"

"He's not here."

"Not here because he's already at the library . . .?"

He swallows as he sticks out his arm for me. "He hasn't returned home since he left after breakfast yesterday."

"Did he say where he was going? Have you looked for him?"

He ignores my questions—or chooses not to answer them. "Gigi, there's someone I would like you to meet."

An old woman, the counterpart to Amorin, marches down the path toward us.

"Pleasure to meet you, Gigi. The name's Clarissa Radley."

"As in *the* Clarissa Radley from Vernal Falls?"

"I don't believe an article is necessary before my name but, yes."

"But you've got to be over a hundred and fifty years old. I mean, you look old but not that old." Then I realize what I said and how insulting it was. What can I say? I can be a real bitch, and backpedaling often causes more problems than just being truthful.

She doesn't appear the least bit offended though. "Oh, I'm much older than that, but how or why is for another time and place. We need to find your father." She spins on her heel and follows a path along the side of the cottage.

"Amorin, Dad is all I have left."

"We'll find him. Have some faith."

I lost faith long ago, but maybe Clarissa and Amorin can aid me to regain some of it.

Clarissa's waiting in Amorin's ceremonial garden for us. When we enter, she grasps our hands so we stand in a tight circle.

"All right, dear, I want you to concentrate on your father's face and focus all your thoughts on him."

I consider his features. His sandy brown hair, his deep brown eyes, his suede-elbowed jackets, his love of old books, his dedication to Druidry, and his love for me—because I know above all else, he loves me. Without intention, though, Alaric's face flashes into my head. His brilliant green eyes, his wavy black hair, his yummy, luscious lips . . . I try to focus back on Dad, but my thoughts keep shifting to Alaric.

Clarissa's warm hand pulses mine. "Who's that boy, Gigi?"

"Sorry. I met him last night. I don't know why I can't get him out of my head."

She breaks the circle and sits down in one of the wooden chairs in the garden. "Not to worry, dear. The sight often comes to us in different ways, and it's up to us to figure out what it's telling us. Besides, as Amorin reminded you earlier, it's the reason why you're here. The boy's awfully cute. What's his name?"

"Alaric."

Amorin takes a seat next to Clarissa. "Young love. What a beautiful thing."

I cross my legs and sit down in the grass. "Love? I just met the guy. I hardly know him. I'm not in love. Did you see Dad?"

Clarissa nods. "I did, but I don't know where he is. He does not appear to be in any immediate danger, so for the time being, I suggest we wait and see."

"You can't be serious. I can't wait for Dad to just show up. He could be in trouble."

She shakes her head. "Dear, he isn't in immediate danger, and for now, that's all we need to worry about."

I shift between anger and disbelief. "Let me get this straight. You're telling me we just wait for Dad to show up? Amorin, are you okay with this?"

"That's exactly what we're suggesting. Life will unfold on its own over the next few days. Now, if I know you, I believe you have some questions for Clarissa."

"Spill it," she says.

I stare at her, trying to decide if I should push the issue of finding Dad, but her eyes hold a firm resolve I know better than to argue with, because it's just like mine.

"What happened the day the boys burned your barn down?"

She blinks back the tears that begin to well in the corner of her eyes. "The day was like any other. I tended to the animals and gardens in the early morning before heading into the woods to collect medicinal herbs and other wild-flowers. I remember sniffing a lilac tree." She stops and smiles at me. "I love the smell of lilacs on a crisp, cool spring morning. But suddenly, as I was sniffing them, a sharp acrid smell rose from the blossoms. My body began to burn all over like it was on fire, and that's when I knew something was wrong. I rushed through the woods to the barn, only to find it completely ablaze. I grabbed buckets of water and tried to douse the flames, but the fire was out of control. I ran to the barn door, but the flames knocked me backward. I heard laughing. Loud, joyous laughing. And that's when I saw the three boys on the hill. I recognized the one boy. I had helped his mother during her pregnancy. He had given her a lot of trouble in the womb, and when I saw him fixated on the fire, I knew why. He was evil to the core, and no amount of love and understanding was going to change him. He must have sensed me staring at him because he turned to me. The sinister glint in his eyes chilled me to the core. At that moment, I knew I had to leave Vernal Falls. It was time to return to Kildare and continue training followers of the Order of Brigit."

"Before you left, did you curse the boys? Is that why they drowned themselves?" I'm curious about the true power of witchcraft.

She shifts in her seat, her hands clutching the armrests. "Dear, I have never once in all my days used dark magic against another living being. Those boys drowned themselves as a result of their own guilt. I had nothing to do with their deaths. No upstanding witch or Druid pursues such a path. Death and destruction will follow evil into the Underworld, but in this world, there is nothing more dangerous than a malevolent witch."

The heat of her anger washes over me, and I know never to cross her, but there's still so much I want to know.

"Why didn't you bring the animals back to life?"

"Child," she says with a heavy sigh, "I do not possess the ability to raise the dead, nor would I, if I did. Once a soul passes, it is best to leave the soul alone. Your grandmother asked that very same question many years ago when she was just beginning to follow Brigit. As you know, she was a seer who loved fiercely. The concept of the Otherworld was new to her, just as it is new to you. She was skeptical of the power of meditation and the ability to connect to those we lose in the Otherworld. I believe she had foreseen that many in her life would die, and she wanted to protect them."

Tears spring to my eyes. Gram's love was equal to none.

"Gigi," Clarissa says, breaking me out of my daze, "I know you don't believe you are Brigit reincarnated, but do you know anything about her?"

I push myself up off the ground. "I think I'll go lie down for a while. I'm a little tired."

Amorin, remarkably fast for his age, stands up to stop me. "Gigi, we're not asking you to believe anything. We just want you to hear her story. It's time your learned about Brigit of Kildare."

"It wouldn't hurt to listen," Clarissa says. "And it could help your Dad and your brother."

At the mention of Scott, I glance over at her. She smiles at me. She knows my weak spot and is not afraid to use it.

I plop back down. "Fine, but it's not going to change anything."

Clarissa winks at Amorin before handing me a delicate piece of fabric. "This tapestry has hung on my wall for many years. It is my most cherished possession."

I carefully drape it across my lap. Along the center, someone embroidered an old woman bent over backward. A young girl emerges from the old woman's stomach, reaching toward a blue sky. Above the old woman's head, the sky is gray and the trees are barren. Over the young girl, birds fly across a sun-shining day. The trees are filled with thousands of blossoms. Along the seams someone embroidered the verse, "As the crone takes her last breath before falling to Earth, the young woman springs forth from the womb, bringing with her the first sparks of life, signifying the end of winter and the return to spring."

"What does that mean?"

"Druidry believes that whatever is, was and shall be. Nothing exists today that didn't exist yesterday that won't exist tomorrow. We are all participants in a never-ending cycle. Birth. Death. Rebirth. This tapestry represents Imbolc, the only Sabbat celebrating the birth of a god."

"What day is that?"

"February 1. Your birthday."

Coincidence.

There are no coincidences.

Great. So Clarissa can inject words into my head. Fanfucking-tabulous.

She looks at the tapestry as if it were a cherished member of her family. "Imbolc, the Festival of Brigit, marks the impending departure of winter and the promised arrival of spring. The days grow longer, and the sun brightens even the gloomiest of places. I spent many cold winter nights weaving the tapestry by firelight when I was a young girl just beginning my training with the Order."

"Following the birth of Jesus Christ," Amorin says, "many areas of the pagan world were plunged into a particularly dark and violent time. 'Missionaries' dispersed throughout the continent to spread the new world of God. Thousands of men, women, and children were killed, and their villages destroyed, because they stubbornly clung to their pagan beliefs. Druid priests and priestesses were beaten, tortured, or burned at the stake for practicing witchcraft. Times were perilous for non-Christians.

"Around 400 AD, a Druid father had a vision he would bring forth a daughter who would shine like the sun and bridge the gap between pagans and Christians. His daughter, Brigit of Kildare, managed to heal the divide by blurring the lines of faith. With Brigit, there is no right or wrong way to honor her. There is only Her. The deaths soon came to an end as Christians and pagans alike embraced Brigit."

Clarissa shifts forward. "But just as the spring maiden grows into the crone, so too did Brigit's time in this world draw to an end. Before she departed, she selected nineteen maidens based on their dedication to her and their adherence to the ancient traditions of Druidry. They became known as the Druid Sisters of the Gallicenial, or the Order of Brigit. On Brigit's final night in physical form, she lit a fire in the sanctuary of the castle. As long as the fire burned, Druidry would continue to exist, thereby demonstrating to the world that her power can never be extinguished or dimmed. For nineteen nights, a different nun tended the Flame. On the twentieth night, they remained in their cloisters and Brigit stood watch. No one knows if she returned physically or if she came in celestial form, but the twenty-day cycle lasted indefinitely."

I didn't notice any thousand-year-old firepit when I was at the ruins. "Does it still burn there?"

"Ireland was invaded many times over the past fifteen hundred years. Much of Druid lore and legend was destroyed. Brigit's Flame was finally doused in the mid-1700s during a Catholic invasion. The Flame was viewed as the remnant of a pagan tradition, which it absolutely was. The invaders refused to compromise their views. During those dark years, the Celtic faith was nearly snuffed out with that fire, but we Irish are a stubborn people," she laughs. "We've managed to keep the faith alive by living on the fringe of society, even going to the new world, waiting for the opportunity to rise again."

Amorin picks at his fingernails as if they're the most interesting thing he's ever seen. "A new flame was lit seventeen years ago in the town center to stand as a symbol of Brigit's lasting impression on this world."

I push up from the ground. "I think I'll go lie down now. I didn't sleep much last night." I return the tapestry to Clarissa's lap. "Thank you both for sharing with me about our past."

I rush away before they can say anything. Even a whisper of reincarnation and I develop the irresistible urge to flee.

22

FAIRY MOUND VISITORS

The splattering of raindrops against the window encourages me to stay in bed, daydreaming about Alaric—his eyes, his smile, his lips. Occasional pangs of guilt rake through me for not thinking of Dad or Scott or Gram or Lizzie or Ryan, but still, selfishly, my thoughts return to him. I've never felt this way about anyone. It's scary as shit but amazing all the same.

A gentle knock comes to my door. "Gigi, I'm heading over to the Cathedral. Would you like to come with me?"

The thought of spending another day among ancient volumes is exceedingly unappealing. "Maybe I'll meet you there later. Is that okay?"

"Perfectly fine, dear. I'll see you back here for dinner."

The front door closes behind him.

As the rain begins to wane, I sigh. I suppose I should go help him. After all, he's trying to figure out a way to save me. I probably should pretend to be interested. Maybe today will be the day he finds whatever it is he's searching for.

On my way over to the Cathedral, a compelling desire to

visit the mound comes over me. There's nothing special about it. Nothing unique. But still it soothes me. I follow the same path I do every day, finding comfort in routine. But today, like most days of my recent life, has proven anything but usual. The light shimmers in a patch of grass so much so that I know it must be something of consequence. I bend down and pick up a smooth shiny blue stone engraved with the triskele on it. The never-ending spiral symbol I had inked on my shoulder without ever having come across it my entire life. And now, it's everywhere, including on a stone on a path I've walked dozens of times since my arrival.

Tracing my fingers along the pattern on the stone, an idea comes to me. I circle the mound once, then twice. I begin to circle a third time when a voice interrupts me.

"I knew you were a siofra! Is this your fairy mound?" Alaric calls out to me.

I freeze. I can't complete my third rotation with his presence.

He saunters over to me. Even his walk is confident and sexy. "You really need to stop following me around," he says. "People will begin to talk."

The flesh and blood of the boy I've been thinking about all day is standing before me, waiting for me to say something.

He reaches for my hand, his touch sending tingles up my arm. "I've left you speechless again, haven't I? I have that effect on women."

"You wish. And I believe you are following me. I was here first."

"True. Maybe I am following you, or you've studied my routine long enough to know that I come here to think. That boulder over there is actually my thinking rock," he says, leading me over to the very rock I've spent my afternoons thinking on. "But you haven't answered my question. Is this your fairy mound?"

I climb up on the rock, and he follows behind me. "Is that what this place is? I've been wondering."

"There are mounds similar to this one scattered all over Ireland. They're believed to be gateways to the Otherworld, but I haven't managed to find the entrance yet."

Curious to find out what he knows about it, I ask, "Otherworld? What's that?"

"Many Irish believe in the Otherworld. Gods and magical creatures of Celtic mythology reside there. A place of great splendor and wonder. You should know. You're from there, aren't you?"

Momentarily stunned, I'm left speechless, which seems to be my typical reaction to Alaric because he's always surprising me. "What . . . what do you mean?"

"You're a siofra. Fairies are from the Otherworld."

"Sorry, I'm from Vernal Falls."

"Sounds like a magical place."

"Vernal Falls? Hardly. There's no magic there." Suddenly, I miss my little corner of my once-stable universe.

"Well, of course not. You're here, aren't you? Now, what are you doing out here all by yourself?"

"Just thinking."

"Something's bothering you. I can tell." He smoothes out the wrinkles on my forehead, his touch sending shivers through me. "Tell me."

I take a deep breath before replying, "I've got a lot of wounds that aren't yet healed."

He cradles my face, catching my eyes with his intense gaze. "Wounds don't heal unless you let them. Let me help you heal," he whispers, casting his spell. "It can't be so bad, can it?"

Entranced, I blurt out my problems without another

thought. "My two best friends just died of rabid dog attacks, my eighty-two-year-old grandmother died suddenly from heart failure, my brother is in jail for a crime he didn't commit, and my father, who came with me to Ireland, has been missing for almost two days. It's pretty bad."

He moves behind me. "Fairies aren't meant to carry such heavy burdens. No wonder you look like you carry the weight of the world on your shoulders," he says as he begins to knead them. I bite my lip, trying not to moan. Between the setting and the masseuse, I'm pretty sure I've found the gateway to the Otherworld as every knot and worry is sated.

"Your smell is absolutely intoxicating to me," he whispers, leaning closer. My body screams for more of his touch.

Slowly, surely, his hands move from my shoulders to my neck sending shivers up and down my spine. "Is there anything else you need, Gigi?" he murmurs, his lips caressing my ear.

Shifting to face him, my eyes fall to his lips. They dance lightly across mine, leaving me waiting. Wanting. When I can't take it anymore, I press my mouth to his. His lips clamp tightly over mine with a fervor rivaling my own as his tongue greedily searches for mine.

His hands tangle into my hair as he pulls me closer to him. The ribbon of air that once existed between us disappears as our bodies intertwine with one another. Driven by pure desire, our touches become more intimate. There is no hesitation. No wavering.

It is as it should be.

A gentle rain begins to fall, but our thirst has not been quenched. We're unable to get enough of each other. My shirt falls open as he pulls the buttons apart. An earsplitting clap of thunder shatters the quiet afternoon. We pull back from one another in surprise as the skies open up, and a deluge cascades down from the heavens followed by another deafening boom.

"Tomorrow," Alaric promises meaningfully.

"Tomorrow," I reply.

Tomorrow.

23

MIDNIGHT VISITORS, AGAIN

*A*fter dinner I daydream by the fire, glowing with happiness as I consider my perfect afternoon with Alaric. I can't help but sigh in contentment at the thought of him.

"I'm pleased to see you so happy, Gigi," Amorin says.

I half smile, staring at the flames.

"Anything you'd like to talk about?"

"No," I sigh. "I just had a very relaxing afternoon."

The flames crackle and hiss as Amorin adds another log to it.

"Clarissa believes Mark will find his way home in a few days. All we can do is wait and continue searching for ways to protect you on Samhain."

"Mm-hmm," I murmur, not really listening to him.

"I'm going to bed. I'll see you in the morning, dear." His hand brushes across my head as he laughs to himself, but I'm too absorbed in my own thoughts to ask him what's funny.

The flames dance before my eyes. The faces of my parents flicker before me. Absentmindedly, I reach into my back pocket and pull out a crumpled piece of paper. Smoothing it out on my lap, I realize it's the map I swiped from the Cathedral my first night in Ireland. With everything that's happened since, I'd forgotten all about it.

Many of the locations on the map are now familiar to me: the Cathedral, the castle ruins, Brigit's Tree, the fairy mound. But there are three more sites I haven't been to yet. There's the round tower on the northeastern border of the map, and in the southeast corner, beyond the castle, the giant bonfire with people dressed in furs dancing all around it. Past that is a square building and several smaller ones clustered around it. I glance out the window. With the moon almost full, I'll have plenty of light to guide me.

I swipe my hoodie off the rack on my way out the door, thinking only about finding my dad. Amorin's sweater brushes my knuckles and falls to the floor. The crumpled pile of wool gives me pause. I've never given much thought about how my actions impact others. I never thought anyone aside from Gram and maybe Dad cared much what I did, but Amorin's panic this morning made me realize that sometimes—most of the time—I can be a real asshole. I hang his sweater back up then scribble a note in case he wakes up and discovers me missing again. I shake my head in disbelief. Ireland is going to destroy my badass reputation.

As I step outside, I take a deep breath. The night air fills me with possibility. I nod at the moon, thanking it for its light, and take off at a sprint. I know—I can't believe I'm running either. I almost veer off in the direction of the fairy mound. I can feel it beckoning me to visit and maybe relive the memory of my perfect afternoon with Alaric. He's like my new drug of choice. I can't get enough of him. He makes me want to believe in "happily ever afters" and "the one," at least for the time being. Ireland is really making me soft-hearted. The kids back home would devour this new Gigi in one bite. Kensey would have a field day. I wonder if she's back in school or if she's still off gallivanting with Breas. Not that I give a rat's ass about him anyway. Especially with Alaric around. Breas doesn't hold a candle to Alaric. He's everything to me.

In the distance, I can just make out the dark outline of the Cathedral. Instead of taking the familiar path that leads toward it, I head southeast toward the square building and the bonfire. Who knows, maybe they'll have s'mores.

I race across the countryside, unafraid of what might be hiding in the shadows. And what shadows there are, disappear with the growing light of the bonfire. As I approach the fire, I recognize the familiar shrouded figure sitting in front of it.

I step into the circle. "Carman."

"I've been waiting for you, dear," she says, her lips moving long after she finished speaking.

"You knew I was coming?"

Gram and I communicated telepathically, Scott a bit, and Lizzie too, but I've never experienced it with anyone else. Someone I don't know.

"Of course. I gave you the book with the copy of the map because I wanted to reveal to you the power of Maleficium, a magic incredibly powerful to combat opposing forces. As a follower of Brigit, you should know these things."

"I'm sorry I took it."

"Dear, it was meant for you since the beginning. It's always been yours."

"You drew the map then?"

"Many years ago." She pauses, finally breaking her gaze from the fire. "Is there anything you'd like to ask me, dear?"

"My father . . . he went missing yesterday. Can you help me find him?"

"It won't be easy. There are certain herbs I need in order to clearly see. They're best collected in the early hours of the day. Come back tomorrow morning and we'll find your dad together. For now, go home and rest. Our journey will require a tremendous amount of energy."

"Thank you for your help, Carman. I am forever in your debt."

"Dear, it's the least I can do for a dedicated follower of Brigit," she says without expression before turning back to the flames.

FILLED WITH ANTICIPATION OF PARTICIPATING IN CARMEN'S magic, but exhausted from my excursion across the countryside, I fall asleep immediately. Not surprisingly, my dreams shift to Alaric and our afternoon rendezvous.

Suddenly, my eyes flash open. The night moon filters into the room, and I make out a shadow looming near my bed.

"Alaric? Is that you?" I whisper, fully believing I'm asleep.

"Gi, I didn't mean to wake you," he whispers in the darkness.

"What are you doing here?"

"I don't know . . . I just found myself by your side when you spoke." There's a quiver to his voice I've never heard before. "I don't feel right," he says as he wraps his arms around himself to calm his trembling body.

I shift over to make room for him. "Sit down."

"No!" He shrieks, backing into the far corner.

"Alaric, what's wrong?"

"I don't know. I need to get out of here." Without another word he leaps through the open window into the night.

In confusion, I scramble to the window and stare out into the darkness. The cold, moist night air cools my face before an earthy hot breeze pushes me back into the room, stinging my eyes. And suddenly I realize, maybe I wasn't dreaming.

24

SPELL WORK AND KISSES

onfused by Alaric's visit, my dreams are haunted by uninvited guests. Finally, after hours of frustration, I kick off my covers and get dressed. Careful not to wake Amorin, I sneak out the front door. It's time to work some magic.

I approach the fire ring from the night before. Small tendrils of smoke slowly creep into the air each time the wind blows. Tall dark pine trees encircle the fire ring, casting almost human-like shadows on the ground that look down-right sinister. Maybe these were the dancing figures on the map, which I mistook for people.

The unsettling feeling of being watched comes over me. Cautiously I call out, "Carman?" as I slowly scan the unfamiliar surroundings. In the distance is the back of a small cottage, a few barns of varying sizes, and a couple of greenhouses. I'm sure this is the cluster of buildings from the map. The garden of the cottage, with its eclectic blend of lawn ornaments including looking glasses, wind chimes, and bird baths, reminds me of Gram's backyard, though it'll never feel the same without Gram.

"Carman?" I call out again.

A loud bang in the nearest barn catches my attention. I head over to the weather-tattered building.

Nothing could have prepared me for the interior of the barn. If I didn't know better, I'd say Carman was a serial killer with a penchant for the weird and furry. It reminds me of Gram's greenhouse because of the hanging bundles of herbs, but that's where the familiarity stops. Instead of shelves of clay pots, Gram's pottery, and other happy gardener objects, these shelves are filled with hooves, antlers, and rabbits' feet. Frogs, mice, spiders, and other creepy-crawlies hang suspended in glass beakers. There are long workbenches, similar to the ones we use for floral arranging, repotting, and cutting, but based on the sharp, grotesquely shaped tools with questionable stains on the tips of them, I'm not so sure I want to know what happens on these tables.

A soft thump draws my attention to a wooden door at back of the barn.

"Carman?" I call out again.

When she doesn't answer, I reluctantly creep toward the rear door, all the while praying some enormous rat doesn't jump out and attack me. Just as I reach the door handle, a loud bang sounding an awful lot like a dropped pot, pulls me back in the direction of the cottage. All too eager to get away from the creepy barn, I head up the worn dirt path.

"Carman, I'm here," I shout as I open the screen door and come face to face with Alaric.

He staggers backward in alarm. "Gigi? What are you doing here?"

"I . . . I . . ." I stutter in astonishment that Alaric is in Carman's house. "Carman told me to come over this morning. I'm . . . I'm sorry to disturb you. I didn't know you lived here."

Now, with time to glance around, I realize it's the same

kitchen he served me breakfast in yesterday morning. An awkward silence follows, neither one of us willing to make the first move or speak the first fumble. Retreat is my best line of defense. Slowly, I begin backing out of the kitchen, but I trip on a floorboard and crash to the floor.

Alaric rushes over. "Gi, are you okay? You're not hurt, are you?"

Tingles run up my arm as he touches it. He gently lifts me to my feet.

I brush myself off, stepping away from him. "I'm fine. I'm fine."

He drags his hand through his hair. "Gi, about yesterday and last night . . ."

Oh god, we're going to have this conversation. He's going to break my heart, and I've had enough of that.

"Don't worry about it. No big deal. Everyone makes mistakes."

He gathers my hands in his. "Gi, it wasn't a mistake. Nothing about you is a mistake."

"I don't understand." Nothing he's saying makes sense, and it's impossible to pay attention to him when I'm trying to ignore the burning sensation in my fingertips.

"You're so adorable when your forehead scrunches up like that," he says, smoothing out the lines as casually as he did the day before. "I followed you into the club. I knew you would be at the mound. Nothing about our meeting is a mistake."

"I don't understand . . ." I whisper.

"Carman is my nan. She wanted us to meet. I told you how she knows things? She knew you'd be in Kildare the other night. I followed you into the club. Into both clubs . . ."

I step away from him. "Both clubs? I've only been to one club since I came to Ireland . . ." I gasp. All the blood rushes out of my head, and I think I'm going to faint. "You . . . It was you at the Metropol . . ." I take a deep inhale and smell the faint trace of cigarette smoke I remember. I don't know why I didn't notice it before. "You, who kept following me around at home, scaring me half to death. You carried me home that night from Radley Pond . . ."

It's as if the world tilts on its axis, and I'm left standing upright. Or, to put it another way, the world remains the same, and I'm knocked on my ass. Literally I fall backward to the floor, spin, and crab crawl out of the room.

"Gi, just wait. Please . . ." he whispers, so softly, so gently, so desperately that I stop moving.

"Nan may have asked me to keep an eye on you, but the moment I saw you I was drawn to you. I felt like my whole life I've been waiting for you. Gigi," he says, grasping my hands, "it's always been you."

His words should terrify me. Send me running for safety. Make me fear for my life. They penetrate into my soul instead. I believe every word. Every damn word.

"She told me to keep my distance. To only watch. But there were times you needed me. That I had to be there for you. You dancing by yourself at the Metropol was the most beautiful thing I've ever seen, and it drew me to you. Then your crumpled body at the lake after that monster left you," he growls, his hands turning to fists. "I wanted to kill him for doing that to you, for hurting you. If he had touched you . . ." he trails off, "I would have stopped him. He wouldn't have laid a finger on you."

He was there all those times, but what about when my friends were in danger? "I needed you up at the church. My friends needed you, and you weren't there for me or them." Tears pool at the corners of my eyes.

He folds his hands in front of him, as if in prayer. "I'm sorry I wasn't there for you. Nan had called me to return home. She foresaw you'd be here soon, and then you were." He stops and smiles at me. A blush creeps up my cheeks.

"I plotted ways I could meet you, but I didn't want to scare you. When you entered the club, I knew it was the perfect opportunity to meet. Then you blacked out, and I brought you back to my place. I know it was selfish of me. I know that I should have taken you home, but I couldn't. Dropping you off yesterday was the most difficult thing I've ever had to do, because now you were real. You make me feel things I've never felt before. After dropping you off, I plotted ways I could see you again. I knew from Nan that you were spending a lot of time at the Cathedral, and I knew you had to pass the fairy mound to get there. I took a chance, and there you were," he says, smiling at me.

I begin to lose myself in his green eyes when suddenly, his face brightens. "Can I show you something?"

"Sure," I sigh, agreeable to anything involving Alaric. Then I remember why I'm here. "I'm supposed to meet Carman. She's helping me with something . . ." Now it's my turn to trail off, because I don't know how much Alaric knows about his nan and Maleficium. I was kept in the dark my whole life. It's possible he was too.

He grabs my hand, sending shivers up my arm. "She won't be back for a few hours. We won't be long."

We run across the sprawling countryside. For once the sun is shining, and the blue skies make everything brighter.

"Where are we going?" I ask, out of breath as I try to keep up with him. I thought I was in good shape after all my walking in Ireland, but compared to Alaric I'm a slug.

"To my favorite place in the entire world. It's a surprise."

"I'm not really thrilled with surprises."

"You'll like this one. Trust me."

The tall brick spires of Saint Brigit's Cathedral become visible in the distance. Instead of turning toward the building, he heads across the fields. The moss-covered stone ruins of the castle grow in mass and height as we pass under Brigit's Tree, but he keeps leading me onward, wandering through several ornamental gardens without stopping.

"Okay, close your eyes," he says.

Putting my faith in Alaric after he confessed he's been following me since Vernal Falls seems foolish, but to me it makes sense. I mean, I've certainly been guilty of poor decision-making in the past, but trusting Alaric seems natural. Seems smart.

"Now, open them."

Several large oak trees encircle us with heavy layers of ivy that hang down from their branches, creating a heavy curtain from the outside world. A small babbling brook gurgles peacefully in the center. Wildflowers, herbs, and lilies blanket the ground. Rays of sunlight shimmer down through the thick canopy, creating sparkles on everything they touch.

"Do you like it?" he whispers. He sounds fearful. Like I won't like it. If he's learned anything these past few weeks of observing me, he should know I love and appreciate objects of beauty.

"I love it."

"I've never taken anyone here. I've never even told anyone about it. I discovered it when I was a little boy. My mom died in childbirth, so my dad was the only parent I ever knew. He used to go away a lot, and I hated it. As I got older, I'd run away from Nan's cottage whenever my dad was about to leave, figuring if he couldn't say goodbye, he wouldn't be able to go, but it never worked. He always found me. Always. No matter where I hid. Until the day I found this place, and I never saw my dad again."

I reach up to touch his face. The pain he feels at the loss of his father physically hurts me. "I'm so sorry about your dad. What happened to him?"

He loops his hands around my hips. "No one knows. Or they're not telling me. I just know he's never come home since that day, and Nan and the rest of them don't talk about him. But never mind that," he says, pulling me under his arm, "I wanted to share this place with you, not give you my sordid history."

"I like learning about you. I feel like I shared so much with you about my life yesterday, that today I should return the favor."

He smiles at me, and I feel at peace.

"So, what is this place?"

"There are sacred wells scattered throughout Ireland—like the fairy mounds. The Druids used to worship at the wells on sacred holidays. When Christianity came to Ireland, nearly all of them were destroyed. There's a well for Saint Brigit close to the Cathedral, but this well is dedicated to the Celtic Goddess Brigit. Her true shrine for her true form," he whispers, gently squeezing my hand. "I don't come here often, but when I do, it gives me the answers I'm looking for. Her presence soothes me, just like yours."

"Alaric, what happened last night?"

"I don't know . . . I was dreaming about you, and suddenly I found myself in your room. I have no idea how I got there . . ." he breaks off, frowning down at me.

"You seemed frightened. Why were you scared?"

"I can't . . . I can't tell you. It's terrible. Twisted." He moves away from me.

I close the space between us and wrap my arms around his waist, pinning him to me. He tries to splinter away, but my grip holds firm.

"I promise I won't be frightened. Please."

"It's terrible. I hate myself for it."

"Please?" I beg again, casting my own spell.

He takes a deep breath, before whispering, "I was staring

down at you, watching you sleep so peacefully, without fear, without pain, just a gentle, peaceful sleep, when an over-whelming surge of loathing ran through me."

"Why?" I murmur, my lips barely moving.

"You awakened in me a hunger I never knew I possessed. I felt completely powerless against you," he whispers.

I can tell how much it pains him to admit these awful truths. I grin, pulling him toward me. "You are completely powerless against me."

He doesn't argue as his lips greedily cover mine, and his strong arms sweep us effortlessly to the soft ground.

Somewhere in the deep inner recesses of my brain, a warning bell goes off again, but I ignore it. When I'm with Alaric, my brain turns to mush and I lose my desire to resist. I've never been so weak, so vulnerable to another's wants. I couldn't say no if I tried.

There's urgency in the air. Tension. Heat. No one will interrupt us here. No one will see us. And with the canopy over our heads and surrounding us, no rain will stop us.

He kisses my neck, and the ability to even think becomes blurry. He teases me with playful bites to my ear, as his hands wander all over my body. Arching my back, I push myself closer to him.

Some primal need pulses through me. I tear off his shirt, my attention drawn to his lean, muscular chest. My fingers explore new territory, causing him to moan. Encouraged by his response, I delve deeper, searching to quench the fire burning inside of me.

Suddenly he breaks away from me and falls back against the ground. "What am I going to do with you?" he moans in a husky voice that's very sexy.

"I can think of a thing or two," I whisper, before nibbling his ear.

"I forget myself with you."

"And that's a bad thing?"

"Yes. I always have to remember who I am, and it's so easy to forget when I'm with you. I'm not who you think I am. There are things about me you wouldn't understand. Things I've done that I'm not proud of."

I stare up at canopy overhead. Slivers of sky break through the thick vines, but blooming moon flowers cover the canopy with a thousand tiny full moons.

"I think I can understand better than most people. There are things about my life that are pretty unbelievable. I haven't lived a normal life by any stretch of the imagination, especially these last few weeks."

"You wouldn't understand this . . ."

I lie across his chest and stare into his green eyes. "Try me. There's more to me than meets the eye."

"That's what I'm afraid of. I'm obsessed with you already. I can't believe I just admitted that . . . I'm afraid that if we do this . . . I won't be able to leave you tonight night."

I pull away from him. "You're leaving? Why?"

His eyes shift to the canopy, as if searching for a reason or not wanting to tell me the truth. "My band's playing out of town tomorrow, and it's a big gig we can't miss."

"Sure, you can," I tease, trailing my fingers along his chest. He rolls away with some effort, but I know it has nothing to do with my physical strength.

"No, I can't. I have to go. And if we do this, I don't think I'll ever be able to leave you."

Talk about a giant confessional time.

"So, don't."

"You don't know what you're asking. I have to leave. I can't stay with you."

"Sure, you can. It's just a show."

His green eyes deepen into sadness. A grim expression passes over his face. "I wish it were that simple," he whispers, holding me tightly. "I promise I will make it up to you when I get back." Then he kisses me along my jawline as he pulls me up along with him. "It's late. Let's get you back to Nan."

ON OUR WAY BACK TO CARMAN'S, I'M FAIRLY CERTAIN MY heart will burst from pure happiness. My whole life I've scoffed at the idea of romance and love at first sight and all that Disney princess crap. I never knew I craved any of it until Alaric came along.

As we approach the fire ring, Carman smiles at us from her chair. "I see you've managed to entertain yourself while I collected herbs."

"Yes, ma'am," I reply respectfully, though she could have been talking to either one of us. "Did you find everything you need? Can I help you with anything?"

"All the herbs are prepared. We will conduct the ceremony tonight with the rest of my coven."

"Tonight? I thought we were going to try and find my dad this morning. I didn't know your coven was coming."

I loathe the idea of involving more people in my affairs.

"With the magic we must conjure, we need a large number of followers." She shifts her attention to Alaric. "I assume everything went well?"

He nods slightly. "Nan, may we speak privately for a moment?"

"Of course," she replies.

"Gigi, I'll be right back," he promises as he follows Carman into the cottage.

I sit down on one of the stumps surrounding the fire pit. Dad's face and my mom's—but not exactly hers—appear in the ashes. I'm sure it's just my imagination, but I blink hard to double check.

The back door slams, breaking my concentration. Alaric moves briskly to my side, grabs my hand, and tugs me away.

"What's wrong?" I ask, trying to keep up with him, but his legs are freakishly long, and he's moving fast.

"Nothing, absolutely nothing."

"Clearly something's wrong. Let's talk about it." I try to stop, but he keeps pulling me forward. "Alaric, you're hurting me. Would you just tell me what's wrong?"

He ignores my pleas until I firmly dig my feet into the ground, bringing him to a halt.

"That's better. Now, what's wrong?"

"Nan and I don't see eye to eye on some things. She wants me to stay tonight and tomorrow night and skip the show."

"I knew I liked her. That's fantastic. So, you're staying?"

"No, I'm leaving. I'll be back the day after tomorrow. Then everything will be fine. I promise." He sounds like he's reasoning more to himself than to me.

Then I realize tomorrow night's Halloween—sorry— Samhain. Old habits. But still, if any of the prophecy is true, tomorrow night might be my last night alive. Tears leak from my eyes again—I really need to get my tear ducts fixed. Even freaky orphans can't feel so damn much. But still, Alaric is leaving, and I may never see him again.

"I'll miss you."

He locks eyes on me. "Gi, it's not forever. It's only for two days, then we'll be together."

A feeling of complete trust overcomes me as I wrap my arms tightly around his waist. As if I want to keep him with me always—which I do.

He chuckles quietly. "You're acting like you're never going to see me again."

"It's because almost everyone I love has disappeared or died these past few weeks. I don't think I can take it if I lose you too."

He reaches down to kiss my forehead. "I will return. There's nothing that will keep me away from you. I promise." He pulls me tightly to him. "Believe me, I don't want to go. I don't want to leave you, but it'll be better for both of us if I'm not here."

I raise my eyebrow. "How can anything be better if you're not around?"

"Trust me. In two days' time, I'll be back with my pockets full of money. Then I'm going to take you out for a proper dinner date. Maybe we'll even hit the club if you promise not to fall asleep again. Does that sound good?"

"Wonderful," I murmur into his chest, so he can't see the tears running down my cheeks.

A harsh male voice catcalls. "So, this is where you've been spending all your time."

Alaric stiffens as he withdrawals from our embrace.

Standing before us is a motley crew of guys. The leader of the bunch leers at me as if he wants to take a bite out of me. His brown hair's disheveled but not sexy like Alaric's. And where Alaric's features are strong and defined, everything about this guy is sharp and angular. His eyes—his eyes are an unnatural shade of yellow that can only come from costume contact lenses. Distaste forms in my mouth. I try to not grimace.

Alaric shifts me behind him. "Declan, what are you doing here?"

Declan peeks over Alaric's shoulder, licking his lips. "Who's your friend? She's positively delicious."

The hairs on the back of my neck stand up as his eyes slowly rake over my body. I curse myself for not wearing more clothing.

"You need to leave now," Alaric warns. A harsh edge coming out of his voice.

"Alac, why so tense? We just wanted to check on our fearless leader," Declan laughs. "Will your friend be joining us on our little trip? I'm sure she'd enjoy our moonlight serenade."

"That's enough, Declan. Get out of here, now."

"Come on, Declan, let's go," a shorter but stockier guy says, pulling at Declan's arm.

Declan feints toward our right. Alaric moves to block him, but before he can recover, Declan lunges to his left. He grabs my arm and pulls me to him, taking an exaggerated inhalation.

A growl erupts from Alaric. I wouldn't be the least bit surprised if fangs protruded from his canines. "Leave her alone. I'm warning you."

His warning sounds like a promise of pain if he's ignored.

"Or what? What are you going to do about it? I just wanted to introduce myself to your friend. Hi, I'm Declan. It's so nice to meet you . . . ?" he says with a question in his voice as he stares at me with those piercing eyes that stab like knives into my soul.

"Gigi Brennan," I murmur, before blinking my eyes and realizing my mistake. His teeth are so blindingly white.

Alaric yanks Declan away from me. "That's enough, Dec," he snarls.

He stares at Alaric, clearly gauging the situation. Alaric is lean and muscular, but Declan's built like a prize fighter. I don't know who would win, and I really don't want to find out.

Finally, after what feels like hours but was probably only seconds, Declan relaxes his stance. "It's all in good fun."

Another guy, who must be seven feet tall, grabs him by the collar. "Come on, Dec, let's go."

"Thanks, Madigan. I'll catch up with you guys later," Alaric says to the group, directing his rage at Declan with the promise to finish what they started.

Declan nods and leads the group away.

I rest my hand on Alaric's back. "What's his problem?"

He immediately tenses. "What? Huh?" he stutters, relaxing his stance when he realizes it's only me touching him. "He's just an asshole who constantly tests my authority over the band."

I can tell there's a lot more he's not telling me, but I still can't get a read on him. I haven't gotten a read on anyone since I've come to Ireland, which is sort of a relief but would come in handy at times like these.

He watches his friends until they disappear over the horizon, and then he keeps watching as if he's certain they're going to come back over the hill.

"Maybe I shouldn't go. But I have to . . . I can't be around here. Is your dad back?"

"Not yet. That's why I went over to Carman's."

"Oh yeah, right. Is someone around to watch over you?" Concern shadows his eyes. I've never had anyone outside my inner circle of family and friends worry about me so much. I can't fully describe the way it feels but nice and refreshing are at the top of the list. Breas dumped me the moment I refused to give in to his desires. It was Alaric that saved me that night too.

Between the spell work tonight and tomorrow night, there will be enough magic to place me up in the tallest tower, and no one will ever be able to hurt me again.

"I'll be with Carman and her coven tonight. Tomorrow night, I'll be home with some family and friends. Does that count?"

Relief washes over him. "Yes . . . good . . . you'll be safe then. Please promise not to leave your house tomorrow night."

"Why?"

"Halloween just isn't safe for young girls to be roaming the countryside by themselves." His demeanor suddenly shifts to sensual as he wraps his arms around my back and pulls me closer to him. "Someone might think you're available."

I eliminate the remaining space between us. "Am I?"

"Absolutely not," he whispers before pressing his lips to mine.

My pulse races as I return the kiss, but then I remember he's leaving for two days, and there's a very good chance I will never see him again. Tears fall down my cheeks, but it's my sobbing that breaks us apart.

"Gi, it's not forever."

"Then why do I feel like I'm playing the part of Juliet?"

He smiles as he wipes the tears from my face. "The difference, dear Gigi, is that we are not characters following an Englishman's storyline for a tragedy. We are in Ireland. We are Irish. We create our own luck. We write our own futures. No one defines us. And by the morning after tomorrow, you will be back in my more-than-capable arms, and nothing will keep us apart. Understand?"

Without waiting for my reply, his lips begin their rhythmic dance over mine, causing any coherent thought or concern to disappear.

A kiss to last through eternity.

25

PRIVATE THOUGHTS

*A*laric left me at the fairy mound with one final kiss and headed in the direction of his bandmates. I think he was worried they'd show up again, or Declan would, and he didn't want him anywhere near me, which is sweet but weird too. I mean, if they're bandmates, why would I be at risk? What terrible acts could Declan be capable of? Not that I really want to find out, but I am curious. You can take The Delinquent out of Vernal Falls, but you can't take The Delinquent out of the girl.

I watched him leave and waited on our boulder for a long time—a very long time—in case he changed his mind and came back to me, but he didn't. I didn't really expect him to. My life has been so full of disappointments. But I thought Alaric might be the one to surprise me. After all, he surprised me this morning at Carman's.

The triskele rock I found at the mound yesterday shifts in my pocket as if to remind me it's still there. I never completed my third rotation after Alaric interrupted me. But his interruption was the best kind. And now, I'm just not

ready to enter another world after not really living a success-
ful, problem-free life in this one.

Amorin's cottage seems the logical place to go. Truth be
told, it's the only place to go, but if Dad's still missing, there
will be no one there for me. And for once I admit it. I need
someone to comfort me. So I go to find the closest thing to
comfort I still have in Ireland: Gram's tea.

After heating up a cup, I curl into a chair and ponder my
day. Chewing the inside of my lip, my eyes settle on a worn
brown leather journal with the initials M.P.O. I pick it up
and turn to the first page, realizing it's Dad's journal. I don't
remember having seen it before. My throat tightens as I leaf
through it, knowing I shouldn't invade his private thoughts,
but I miss him too much not to.

According to the date on the first page, he started it
twenty years ago around the time he first met Calliope.

~MET AN ENCHANTRESS TODAY. BLACK HAIR, ICE-BLUE EYES,
pale white porcelain skin, an exotic beauty blessed by Brigit
herself. Her name is Calliope Brennan. She hails from Vernal
Falls, Pennsylvania, in the United States. She's the daughter
of the well-known and respected High Priestess, Rose
Brennan.

I SKIP A FEW PAGES TO AVOID ANY POTENTIAL GRAPHIC
content surrounding his relationship with Calliope. I know
too much about his sex life already. Some red ink in a
different hand catches my eye.

~A PROPHECY MADE BY CALLIOPE BRENNAN, SO IT IS SURE TO
be blatantly ignored.

A broken heart turns to black.
Love forsaken. Hunger awakened.
Consort with lunar pull.
Taken in by ravenous thirst.
Revenge blinded.
Others' will irrepressible.
Chaos and destruction to ALL inevitable.

ANOTHER RIDDLE TO FIGURE OUT. I HATE FUCKING RIDDLES.

Whose heart turns to black? Mine? Because that's completely believable. I'm fairly certain it is already. Calliope's? Also possible, and she's dead, so that's a win. Someone else's? Maybe. Hopefully Celtic mythology doesn't have a Medusa figure. We've had enough gods reincarnated recently, and we certainly don't need any evil ones. And the whole, "Love forsaken, hunger awakened" line can't be good. There's nothing worse than a woman scorned in love, especially if hunger's involved. Is it hunger for power, for love, for food?

And I definitely don't like the whole "Chaos and destruction for ALL inevitable," because "ALL" in capital letters makes me think the whole world's in trouble. Between two dead bffs, a brother in jail, a missing dad, a boy I may never see again, and, oh yeah, a lunatic werewolf after me, I've got enough on my plate.

Let's move on.

~ARRIVED IN VERNAL FALLS TODAY. CALLIOPE DECIDED SINCE she's pregnant with our first child that she'd like to move home to be close to her mother and sister. Rose Brennan is every bit the firecracker she was described to be, and her daughter Lulu is a mirror image of her.

. . .

I STOP AND CONSIDER WHAT DAD WROTE. CALLIOPE AND Lulu were identical twins, so they were mirror images to each other, but then, why did he mention Lulu as the mirror to Gram and not Calliope? Was it more in action and attitude rather than appearance? Because I know that in many ways I, too, look like my mom, except for the black hair underneath, which mirrors Calliope's hair. I never considered myself a younger version of Gram, though maybe I am. A part of her is with me. That gives me incredible peace.

Anxious to read more about Dad's first impressions of my mom, I flip the page only to discover that many of the pages that follow are either erased, blackened, or torn out. Not knowing if the journal was altered by Dad or someone else, most likely Calliope on a jealous rampage, I continue searching for answers I didn't even know I had questions for.

~GIGI, MY BEAUTIFUL DAUGHTER WAS BORN AT HOME TODAY with Rose serving as the midwife. She is the most precious little angel I've ever seen and just as smart too. She grabbed my finger when I stopped in to visit and smiled. Actually smiled. It tears my heart that I can't take more of a fatherly role in her life. I am relegated to "dear uncle" for fear others will discover who Gigi really is. Protecting my little girl is our number one priority. Nothing else matters.

BLINKING BACK THE TEARS, I REALIZE THE EXTENT OF MY family's sacrifice. They all dedicated their life to keeping me safe without expecting anything in return. I will not let them down. Not that I in any way believe I am Brigit reincarnated

—no goddess would be such a fuck-up—but I will do what I can to honor their sacrifice.

The dates in the journal grow more sporadic. Some entries go on for several pages, while others are only a sentence or two. I take center stage in the content, with Scott playing a supporting role.

~WOUNDED CATS AND DOGS, ALONG WITH NUMEROUS OTHER animals, have shown up at Rose's doorstep. One-year-old Gigi, who is already walking, toddles out and rubs different poultices and salves on them from Rose's apothecary kit. Once she's done, they lick her and go on their way or decide to adopt Rose and Gigi as their new family.

~CAN'T BELIEVE THE FRUITS AND VEGETABLES HARVESTED FROM Lulu and Rose's garden this year. They've been canning for weeks, along with giving basketfuls away to coven members and neighbors. Either they've developed a green thumb, or the additions to our family have led to a fertile ground.

BUT IT'S THE NEXT ENTRY, STAINED AND CRUMPLED, THAT catches my attention.

~DEVASTATION STRUCK. LULU GONE. CLAYONE IMPRISONED. Lulu gone.

DAD'S FEW SHORT WORDS CRY OUT ABSOLUTE DEVASTATION, but it's what he didn't write that destroyed him the most.

In contrast, the next entry is devoid of emotion.

. . .

~CALLIOPE IS GONE. SHE COULDN'T TAKE THE RESPONSIBILITY of motherhood or the responsibility of her actions. Her betrayal of Gigi and Lulu, of all of us, consumed her with well-deserved guilt. Maybe she got what she deserved for all the pain she caused.

IN ALL MY YEARS OF KNOWING DAD AS OUR FRIENDLY neighbor, affectionately called "Uncle Mark," I have never heard him speak or act in such a bitter, hurtful manner. The pain Calliope caused my family must be punished. If she were alive today, she'd be scared shitless, because my violent side would be put into action. No one hurts the ones I love. No one.

From then on, the entries revolve around me.

~AT THREE YEARS OLD, GIGI CONDUCTED HER FIRST SUMMER solstice ceremony. All eyes of the coven watched her with pure love and affection. She glowed in the circle as she spoke, so much so that we know it couldn't be just a trick of light. Rose and I have decided to shield Gigi and Scott from our practice. When they are older and can fully understand Gigi's role and Lulu's sacrifice, then we will tell them the truth and reveal to them the wonders of Druidry and our connection to Earth. Until then, may they live in peace and contentment. Ignorance surely is bliss.

~NANCY AND GREG CAME OVER AND INFORMED US THAT THEY no longer want to be a part of the coven, and Gigi is no longer welcome at their house. When I asked why, they told me that when Gigi was playing with Lizzie, she formed a fireball between her fingers and lit some candles. Evidently, thinking she's a goddess and actually seeing her put her gifts into action are much different. They see only danger and devil's work rather than the beauty of it. Gigi will be devastated. She adores Lizzie. They've been playmates since their birth.

Rose and I have decided to up her dose of tea in order to stave off her powers. The protection ceremony will need to be held at the Beltane ceremony rather than Lughnassad in order to lay additional enchantments on her so she doesn't begin to see or develop her powers.

Lizzie's parents were afraid of me. That's why they acted like I was the devil. "That thing," her mother screamed at me. And now I know why. They heard the prophecy. They either believed I was a goddess or would be targeted because everyone believed me to be one, and in some way I'd one day put Lizzie in danger. I don't even remember us together when we were younger. I thought it was only Scott and me. Did Gram and Dad wash our memories away, or did the tea do it? No wonder when Lizzie and I met in second grade in Mrs. Fury's class it felt like we had known each other forever. We had.

I stare at my fingers. Did I really make fireballs with them? I study each tip and think fire thoughts, but nothing so much as a spark comes out. I tilt the contents of my mug and watch the stray tea leaves swish back and forth. Gram never shared with me all the herbs she blended for my tea, and now I know why. She used magic on me to suppress my supposed powers. What would happen if I didn't drink the tea? Could I shoot fireballs then? What else am I capable of?

I skip a few pages, not really wanting to read more of the

Gigi-the-Goddess-did-this-wonder, before continuing . . .

~For Scott's seventh birthday, the coven bestowed on him a silver dagger, heavily enchanted with protective charms. The dagger will be worn around his ankle at all times. Gigi will receive a silver bullet on her seventh birthday. The bullet is drilled at the base and will serve as a good-luck charm for her. The silver talismans will cast a spell over them to further prevent them from seeing as their grandmother and Lulu did. They cannot see the future yet. We must protect them for as long as we can. Gigi cannot know she is Brigit reincarnated. Scott and Gigi need to live a worry-free life until the time presents itself.

I let the journal fall to my lap. Huh, I wonder what that's supposed to mean. Dad had no idea I could release Clayone. Neither did Gram, or they would never have let us camp out in the woods so close to Clarissa's farm. What future is he alluding to? What type of dangers did he foresee?

Amorin bursts in. "Gigi, I have news. Wonderful, incredible news!"

His excitement blasts at me like a rush of electricity, but it doesn't even crack my surface. So much has been kept from Scott and me. I wish Scott was here. To talk to. To just be there for me. I need him more than I ever realized. With him around, I never needed to be strong or brave. He shot his best friend to protect me and got locked away because of it. And now I face Amorin and his "news" alone.

"What is it?"

"There was a third protective spell cast by Brigit to help werewolves!"

I'm not sure how helping a werewolf will save my life

tomorrow night, but let's see where this goes.

"Where did you find it?"

"In Brigit's ruins," he says, circling the room as if he can't contain himself. "Do you remember the stone tablet with the Celtic cross on it? The one with the triskele?"

No. I hadn't noticed it. I finger the rock in my pocket, feeling the never-ending spirals that Kildare is filled with.

Without waiting for my response, he continues. "After a visit to the Otherworld this morning, I wandered out to the ruins in search of a particular stone."

I lean forward, remembering the stone I had wanted to examine. Or rather, move. Could it be the same one?

"Beneath it there was a vault containing a pile of old annals, probably as old as the ruins themselves. Annals are essentially journals the monks used to record information. They had a tendency to hide information in surprising places to ensure that, while the church did not support Druidry or witchcraft, the information would not be lost forever. Embedded in a recipe for buttercream biscuits, I found the third spell. I should have guessed there was a third spell, because the number three is sacred to Druids. But no matter, we know now. There's a herb, nightlock, that anyone bitten by a werewolf can wear around his or her neck during a full moon. If the herb is worn, the victim will not turn into a werewolf. Isn't that brilliant?"

His enthusiasm does nothing to help mine. I set my tea down, stand up, and head to my room. I am so incredibly tired.

He must sense I'm in no mood for conversation because he stops talking. I close the door behind me, fall to the bed, and stare at the ceiling with its cracks and patches. If I'd had that herb, Ryan would be alive. Knowing I could have prevented Ryan's death is a terrible blow to my already with-ered self.

26

LOVE POTION NUMBER

$\mathcal{H}$eaviness hangs in the air on my return to Carman's. Amorin left a note telling me he returned to the ruins to read more of the annals and that if I was feeling up to it, I could join him. Breathing seems like a chore with my heart so heavy. Even from a distance, the fire is a clear indication that tonight will be unlike any other. Green and blue flames pirouette into the night sky with Carman as the conductor. The ceremonial ring hosts a crowd of unfamiliar faces, causing uneasiness to settle over me. I cast a cursory glance around, hoping that Alaric changed his mind, but he didn't. I am alone.

"Gigi, dear, it is so good to see you," Carman says from across the fire.

I nod my head dutifully, unsure where I should go.

"Stand over by me. I'll need to connect with your energies in order to find your father."

In the middle of the fire, a large black cauldron churns a fluorescent green concoction. Is that what real magic looks like?

"Gigi, we just need a hair from your head to begin."

I place one in her cold, shriveled hand.

When she drops the hair into the cauldron, the liquid immediately boils, seething with anger. She begins to chant, and the brew dances to the rhythm of the incantation. Soon the coven members join in. I try to catch what they're saying, but it's in a foreign tongue, and although I seem to always understand ancient Gaelic, they're speaking something else entirely.

The flames grow higher and higher as they chant. A vision of Dad locked in a tower looms before me. A full moon slides into the small window. Calliope and Scott are with him, but I know that my vision must be distorted. Calliope is dead. Scott is safe in jail.

Dad turns to me and says, "Gigi, do not—"

Abruptly the vision cuts off. I stare at the flames in disbelief.

"Was that real?" I whisper into the fire.

"Oh yes, dear. Your father is locked in a tower somewhere, and you're the only one who can find and free him. The moon was full in the tower window. You must go when the moon is at its lunar fullness. Do you know when that is?"

"Tomorrow night."

"You are correct."

"I saw my brother and his mother too."

"Thoughts, dear, only thoughts. You've probably been thinking about your brother since you've been away from each other. It's only natural his mother would be at his side."

"Dad started to talk to me. He said, 'Do not . . .' but he was cut off."

"Ah, yes, we are so anxious to see the ones we care about that we often project messages into our own minds. But visions cannot speak to us . . . they merely provide a picture. It is up to us to discover the answers." She gently pats me on

KB ANNE

the back, but it does nothing to relieve my anxiety over the appearance of my brother or Calliope.

She spreads her arms out, as if pulling everyone to her. "Does anyone else have a request?"

One female member about my age with mousy brown hair squeaks, "I want Elijah to fall in love with me."

"Do you have the sacrifice?"

The girl produces a piece of hair and an article of clothing from her bag. She hands it over to Carman. Carman passes her a piece of straw before taking a cold, calculating look at me, as if assessing my reaction to what's about to occur.

"The boy's full name?"

"Elijah Murphy."

"Elijah Murphy, Elijah Murphy," she chants, throwing the girl's sacrifice into the fire, "Let your heart dance before Marie Donahue. She will control the strings, and you will obey every whim." Then she murmurs something so low I miss it, though I'm standing right next to her. She turns to Marie and indicates the fire with a grand sweeping of her arm. Marie touches the straw to her heart, then to her lips, before tossing it into the fire. The straw bursts into flames. Slender tendrils of smoke glide into the air before disappearing into the darkness.

"Any other requests?" Carman asks the crowd.

A male, around thirty years old, steps forward. "My wife's been fornicating with Alexander McConnell. I want them to pay."

Carman contemplates him. The anger in his tight white fists, his stiff shoulders, and his clenched jaw all point to revenge, which he'll get one way or another.

"Tonight is not a night of retribution. Tonight we celebrate the possibility of a different tomorrow, the possibility of new beginnings."

The man opens his mouth to argue with her but stops

when Carman silently chants something. His eyes bulge out of his head, and he immediately withdraws from the circle.

For the remainder of the evening, visions dance before me. I witness spells ranging from healing ones to promises of good fortune. Power swirls in the air around Carman. She grows younger as the flames lick the sky, yet no fuel has been added. For the first time since discovering that witches, werewolves, and magic are real, I witness true power, and its name is Maleficium. If I could harness it, I could defeat Clayone. I would never sleep in fear again. I would no longer need to remain wide awake.

27

BLOOD SUCKERS

*A*morin knocks at my door entirely too early. I am by
no stretch of the imagination ready to wake up and
face this day. He peeks in.

"Gigi, child, we need to begin the preparations for this
evening. Are you ready?"

"Mm-hmm," I mumble, stretching my sore limbs.

"Late night last night?"

Again, I mumble something resembling, "Mm-hmm, I'll
be out in a few minutes."

"Take your time. Clarissa and several coven members are
here. More are on their way over."

Pulling the blankets over my head and going back to sleep
sounds like the smartest way to spend this day, but a sense of
obligation to Gram and Scott, to Mom and Dad, to even
Lizzie and Ryan, overshadows my desire to sleep. Coven
members have traveled from all over the globe for this night.
For me. I must not let them down. Tonight, I will play the
role of goddess, and when the werewolf army doesn't take
over the world, they'll realize they put their faith in the
wrong girl.

Before joining everyone outside, I head to the kitchen to make some of Gram's tea. Habit I guess. Now that I know I've been spelled, I'm not sure I should drink it. Will my powers reveal themselves in a giant fireball if I stop drinking it? I smell the loose tea leaves. The scent reminds me of her, and today of all days, I need the comfort of my gram. I decide to brew a cup. Just one more, I say to myself, but I know I'll drink it until the blend is gone and Gram disappears with it.

After my first sip, the soreness in my arms and legs slips away as the healing powers of the herbs seep into my bloodstream. But I still don't feel myself. An intense heat radiates off me, even though the cottage is freezing. I wrap a blanket around me as a robe before shuffling out to the garden. Maybe I'm coming down with the flu.

When Clarissa sees me, she drops the basket she's carrying. Herbs fly in every direction. The other people gasp at the sight of me—which is pretty freaking rude considering they think I'm a reincarnated goddess and they're acting like I'm spewing green bile out of my mouth as my head spins in circles.

"Gigi, what happened to you?" she cries, rushing over to me.

I back away from her, knocking into Amorin. He quickly grabs me before I can get away.

"Where were you last night?"

"I was at a friend's house."

She presses her fingers into my forehead. Warmth radiates from them. "What friend? What were you doing?"

I try to pull away from Amorin's grasp, but he's surprisingly strong for an old guy. Eventually, when Clarissa releases her voodoo touch, he lets me go.

I step away from them. "What's the big deal? What's wrong with me?"

A woman I don't know thrusts a mirror in front of my

face. A freak stares back at me. My pupils have all but removed even a trace of the aquamarine of my iris. My cheeks are pinched and hollow. It's like my skin shrank, and my skull is too large for what's left. Tentatively, I reach up to touch my face, not trusting the mirror.

"You witnessed sorcery last night, didn't you?" Amorin says.

"No, I was with Alaric last night. We had a campfire and stayed up late. I'm just tired and probably having a reaction to the smoke or something."

Like searing the lining of my larynx.

Clarissa and the rest of the coven members stare at me. I can tell they don't believe a word I'm saying. I may not be able to read their minds, but their facial expressions reveal everything I need to know.

"What's the big deal anyway?"

"Sorcery is extremely powerful dark magic," Clarissa says. "It creates doubt in people who don't believe in the power of meditation. It's a shortcut, and there is a great price for those who follow it—at their demise, their souls will be cast down to Derg in the Underworld instead of entering the Otherworld. They forfeit all chances of reincarnation. Followers of dark magic manage to keep themselves alive way beyond their life expectancy by sucking the life from the living. From the pure. Your face bears the mark of exposure." She reaches up to touch me again. I back away from her.

"I'm having a reaction to the smoke or dust or something. I had no exposure to sorcery, nor did I give anyone permission to suck my blood. Besides, I'm not pure anyway. No one would benefit from sucking anything from me."

She studies me. "They don't suck your blood, child. They suck your life force, and yours is terribly weakened."

I go almighty goddess on them by lifting my chin, sticking out my chest, and speaking in a manner that suggests I'm enlightened. It's a crock of shit, I know, but they leave me with no choice. "My life force is fine. Now, if you'll excuse me, I need to tend to some things before this evening."

Amorin and Clarissa, along with the rest of the coven, watch me leave. I'm struck with the irony that the two people who believed in me the most, Gram and Dad, would never have let me go, but they're not here. Meditation and chanting did not bring my Lizzie back from the dead, or stop Ryan from turning into a werewolf, or even keep Gram alive. If I spent decades learning Druidry and studying with the Order, maybe I'd believe their way would work, but I didn't, and I don't. I witnessed the power of Maleficium last night. With it, I can save my dad. With it, I can defeat Clayone. And if it means I will be cast into the Underworld without the chance of reincarnation, so be it.

28

TOWERING DISCOVERIES

*M*y vision revealed Dad was locked in a tower. According to the map, there's a large, round tower along the northeastern outskirts of Kildare. It's the only place I haven't been to yet, and while it would be remarkably convenient and easy if he was there, I'm not going to hold my breath. My life has never been that simple. Carman said I should wait until evening, but I made a promise to Alaric, and for once I plan to keep it.

Age and elements have worn away the yellow stone blocks of the tower, creating a pockmarked exterior surface. Moss and ivy took up residence long ago, giving the stone a weird otherworldly glow. It is as if the tower grew out of the earth. There's not a door or a visible entrance that I can see around the base of it. If I asked Rapunzel to let down her fair hair, I wonder if she'd oblige.

Around the back side of the tower, there's large stone that could be a door. I press on it and realize it's not stone at all. It's a thick wooden door painted to blend in with the stone block, and there's a small hole where a key or a handle must go. I wedge my finger into it and pull, but my pinkie, while capable of miraculous thievery at times, does not wield a force mighty enough to open it. Kneeling in front of the door, I scour the ground for a stick or rock I can wedge into it. Then I remember the stone I found at the fairy mound. It's just the right size for the hole. I unwind one of my wire necklaces and wrap it around the stone. Lizzie showed me an unlocking spell when we were looking through the spell book weeks ago. At the time, I was only thinking about breaking into Kensey's house and stealing something of hers just to mess with her head, but maybe it'll work now.

I begin chanting in Gaelic, waving the makeshift key over the door around and around. When the stone warms and begins to glow, I place it in the door and pull. The door creaks and moans, shifting and sagging, until it finally opens. Before entering, I withdraw the stone and hold on to it, letting its warmth and light fill me with courage. I glance behind me to ensure I wasn't followed.

The soft glow of the stone casts enough light for me to see inside the tower. In my vision there was a window, but it's only midday and there's no evidence of a window anywhere. I climb the rickety stairs, holding tightly to the railing. Angry creaks and bellows follow me all the way up. I hope the steps are strong enough to hold my weight on the way down or it'll be a quick, neat death for me. At the landing there's another door, which is also locked. I wave the stone key and chant again. The stone glows bright, and I hear the gentle click of the internal locking mechanism. The unlocking spell will come in handy when I go home, and Lizzie and I could . . . Then I remember I will never do anything with Lizzie ever again because she's dead, and I need to accept that. And I would, except for the fact that I am stubborn and I refuse to acknowledge that she's gone forever. If I can find the Vessel of Life, I can bring her back. I can bring them all back. Voldemort split his soul every time he killed someone and placed it in a Horcrux. I'll do the reverse—bring everyone I love back to life and split my own soul in the process. My soul for their life? That's not even a contest.

Something or someone moves inside the room. The window from my vision casts a dim light, and there in the shadows is Dad, chained to the floor. A foul smell fills my nostrils. His captors didn't even allow him to use a bathroom —the monsters.

"Dad," I shout, running over to him.

"Gigi, my little girl, what are you doing here? I told you not to come."

His admonishment hurts me more than a punch ever could. "I thought that was just a dream. Carman said messages are only in the mind."

"Carman is the one who put me in here." His voice sounds dry and hoarse, not at all like himself. "Gigi, listen to me. Calliope is alive. She has Scott."

The wind knocks out of me. "He's not supposed to be here. He's supposed to be safe in juvie. She's supposed to be dead."

He reaches for me, but the chains don't allow him much freedom. I move over to him. His touch fills me with warmth.

"Calliope must have brought him over after we left. She and Carman are working together."

Another punch.

"They're evil witches who practice Maleficium—sorcery —the most powerful type of dark magic there is."

Bile climbs up my throat. "Maleficium is dark magic?"

"The worst type of dark magic. Listen to me. They're planning something huge. I think they want to bridge the gap between our world and the Otherworld, and tonight, with the Super Blue Blood Moon on the lunar eclipse, they can do it. They can release the Fomorians, the most terrible demons that ever walked the Earth. I think they're trying to bypass Clayone completely."

"Why would they do that?"

"To throw the world into chaos. They want dominion over every living creature. There's too much to explain. You need to get back to Amorin's and do what they tell you. Our prime objective tonight is to protect you from Clayone. No one else matters. Do you understand?" He searches my eyes.

Clayone's thousands of miles away. Dad must be completely delusional.

"What about you?"

"What about me? I am everything to them because of you, but I am nothing to them if they can't get you. Amorin and Clarissa know where I am. They've known since I went missing."

The stab of betrayal rushes through me. "What? They lied to me."

"Gi, they just didn't share their knowledge with you. They'll come for me tomorrow. But tonight you need to go to them and let them protect you. Now go, before someone comes."

"I can't leave you."

"Carman and Calliope mustn't get to you, or you will be sacrificed. Now go," he says ripping his hands from mine.

"Dad, I can't," I whimper, throwing my arms around him.

"You can, and you must. Don't worry about anyone but yourself. Stay safe. Now go," he says.

"Dad . . ."

"Go. We don't have much time."

"Dad . . ."

His eyes tear up. "Gigi, if you love me, you will do this for me."

I blink back my own tears and disappear down the stairs.

Upon exiting the tower, I search the horizon for potential enemies. The clear blue skies give no hint of the terrible storm brewing.

I take a deep breath and run. Not in the direction of Amorin's, but to prepare for battle. There's only one way to protect the ones I love . . .

I need to ask the real Brigit for help.

29

TALLEST TOWER TRAPPINGS

*N*o one followed me from the round tower, or if they tried to, they'd be shit out of luck. I wound through the streets of Kildare as if I had spent my life wandering through the town. I slipped down alleys, trespassed across people's backyards, and climbed over fences. No way, no how, did anyone follow me. I even stopped once in a while and stood watch so if anyone was following me, they'd get a face full of pepper spray.

Slipping the triskele-engraved stone from my pocket to my hand, I circle the fairy mound, three times clockwise, then three times counterclockwise. I close my eyes and plead for divine assistance from the one person who can help me: the true Brigit.

"The time has come to lend a hand. Please allow me to enter in order to find instruction. If shown the way, I cannot fail. Believe in me, as I have come to believe in you."

A heavy fog, warm and inviting, blankets the valley as two white stone columns with an archway materialize before me. I glance backward once before entering, but I don't need to worry about being followed here. The thickness of the fog will obscure the view of anyone watching. As the fog envelops me, the rules of Earth's gravitational pull lift, and my body becomes weightless.

My spiritual journey with Amorin to the Otherworld did little to prepare me for the splendor before me now. Captivating emerald-green landscapes, mesmerizing azure blue skies, and a timeless wonder permeate as if the very air is alive. And maybe it is. Every sense is heightened. The air smells sweet and delicious, leaving me content and sated like I just ate a fulfilling meal, though I can't really remember the last time I ate. The quiet babble of water far in the distance calls me to discover its source, but the hedge maze looms before me, far more formidable than in my previous spiritual visit. With my vision crystal clear, it's almost as if the path through the maze is already laid out for me, and there is nothing to do but follow it.

Turning on instinct at each intersection, I follow along confidently, but as I venture deeper into the maze and the minutes tick away and there's no hope of retracing my steps, I start to panic. I mean, who am I kidding? Do I really believe that I'm actually capable of getting through the maze, learning what I need to while there, and returning in time to save Dad? It's ridiculous. Idiotic. It's . . .

I round the final corner and the courtyard presents itself to me, amazing.

I made it. I actually did it.

The small courtyard hosts a lovely garden of butterfly bushes, phlox, bee balm, and foxglove, along with dozens of other familiar herbs and wildflowers. Under normal circumstances, the gardens would beckon me to stop and investigate, but today far more important matters require my attention. An intricately carved granite foundation with a delicate sculpture of a green-hued copper fairy features prominently in the heart of the courtyard. As I approach, the fairy winks at me then tilts her head to the bench on the other side where Gram and Mom wait for me.

My throat catches at the sight of them. For the first time in my life, I truly see my mom—an exquisitely featured woman whose love emanates a dazzling glow to behold. Beside her sits Gram, indeed a mirror image of her daughter caught ageless in the Otherworld.

"We knew you were coming," Mom says, indicating the large worn leather volume on the bench with the pale gold lettering. *Briguathe Grimoire*. The book from my vision with Amorin.

Raw emotion, pure and primal, surges through me, making it difficult to speak. I finally whisper, "Mom, I'm sorry. I had no idea what I was doing when I released Clayone."

Her hands—her warm soft hands—reach up and cradle my face as her blue eyes stare lovingly into mine, and I remember what it felt like to be an infant in her arms and even before, when she carried me in her womb. I remember everything.

There's so much I want to say to her. So much I want to ask. So much of *everything* I don't even know where to begin, except that I know there isn't time for lovely reunions. There's no time *period*.

"My Gigi, my love, my life. My sacrifice is nothing compared to yours. Are you sure you want to follow through with your plan?"

The power of mind reading greatly diminishes the need for lengthy conversation.

Tears form at the corner of my eyes. Never have I felt so much love. It's like my heart will burst. It's like I will burst. "I don't see any other way. I must protect the ones I love. Nothing else matters. Is Brigit here? Will she help me?"

Gram embraces me, whispering, "She's here. She's always been here."

I break away to search for the Goddess, but no one's there, and I realize that Gram's back to her Gigi-is-the-Goddess delusions.

"They are not delusions, and what you plan is a huge gamble. I don't think you should take it. We are all willing to sacrifice our lives for you."

I blink back tears and swallow hard. "I know, but I'm not willing to let everyone sacrifice their lives for me. Which ones should I use?"

Mom pats the space next to her, and the three of us leaf through the book together. The pages spring to life, presenting various spells and incantations. Most of them assist the harvest or heal someone who's hurt. There's nothing about fighting lethal enemies. I practice calling the wind a few times, wondering if the wind can possibly be of use to me. I cast a protection spell on my trusty old silver bullet, hoping I have the strength to thrust it into Clayone if he should show up tonight, though he is the least of my worries. He's most likely roaming the mountains around Vernal Falls, waiting to strike—Imagine his surprise when he realizes I'm gone. All his careful planning and preparation, and I'm thousands of miles away. That will be sweet justice.

I murmur a binding spell that will bind any evil to me. As I practice, Gram interrupts my chanting.

"Be careful with binding spells. Especially evil-binding spells. They are particularly draining. If you bind Carman to you, you won't have the strength to protect yourself. Use the spell only as a last resort."

"Yeah, sure," I agree, but I know she can read my mind. She knows I'll use it regardless of what she says.

After studying a few more spells, the sun still high up in the sky, Mom clucks her tongue. "It's time to go or you will be locked in the Otherworld forever. As much as we would love that, we know there's still work for you to complete."

Gram places a bundle of dried plants in my hand. "This herb is for you. Hold onto it for the time being. It won't help you tonight, but if all goes well, it will save lives in the future."

I clutch the herbs to my chest, knowing that she's not telling me everything, but this time I don't feel like fighting for more information. These final moments might be the last time I'll ever see them again. If Clayone should find me or if Carman destroys me, I will be cast to the Underworld forever.

They both smile at me with so much love it overwhelms me. Mom whispers, "We will be together again, one way or the other."

If I let myself think about their love or what's happened or what I have planned, I might break down and be unable to carry out my plan, so I turn away and step into the fountain. The fairy winks at me, and I step out of the sacred well at Alaric's secret spot. Through the canopy of vines, I can see the darkness. The moon flowers are in full bloom, and day has shifted into night. I sprint in the direction of the round tower, praying I'm not too late.

After the door opens at my entrance spell, I realize something's different.

"Gigi, it's a trap! Get out now!" Dad yells from above, just as filthy hands grab my arms.

"So nice of you to join the party," cackles a disgusting ogre of a man. His foul breath alone could kill someone.

"Calliope and Carman will be so pleased you decided to join us after all."

He tries to force me up the stairs. I punch and claw, refusing to cooperate. But he's not deterred. He throws me over his shoulder and climbs the stairs while I kick and scream. If there is a god, our combined weight will break through the rotted wood and we'll plummet to our deaths. But I have no such luck.

At the top of the steps he stomps across the landing and into the room. I never closed the door. That's how he discovered I'd been there. That's how he knew I would return. He tosses me onto the floor next to Dad, shackling my arms and legs.

"Just in case you try to escape. Calliope will be here shortly to bring you to the ceremony this evening. You two are the guests of honor." He cackles on his way back down the stairs.

Dad nudges me with his shoulder. "Gigi, I told you not to come. I am willing to sacrifice myself for you."

"I know," I whisper, "but I'm not willing to sacrifice you."

Tears stream down my face. Stupid tears for a stupid idiot. I am so stupid. So fucking stupid. For the first time since Lizzie's funeral, I let myself cry for all those I've lost and will lose from my own ignorance. With no ability to wipe the tears away, they roll down my face and onto my fettered wrists.

The last colors of sunset disappear from the horizon. Soon, the moon will be full.

"Gigi, look."

Vines begin wrapping around our iron shackles, prying them apart.

"What the devil?" the guard cries out. "What kind of hocus pocus are you working up there?"

We stare wide-eyed at each other as our chains fall away. Without a word, we climb down the stairs. At the bottom, the vines have twined around the guard, holding him in place.

We slip into the night. I beckon Dad to follow me to Carman's house. "We have to find Scott."

He grabs my hand, pulling me in the opposite direction. "We need to get help. We can't do this alone. Wait—someone's coming."

Before I can see who it is, he pulls me behind a grove of oak trees. The open spaces blur into the trees, and we are completely camouflaged. It's probably a trick of the light, but after all I've seen, it might just be magic.

We watch a lone woman approach the tower. Calliope. Her appearance now unmistakable. She was the woman from the flames. The woman who betrayed her family. The woman who killed my mom. Anger boils through me. I prepare to spring up and confront her, but Dad pulls me back.

"She knows where Scott is."

Nodding, I grit my teeth.

We watch her enter the tower. A scream fills the space between us. She reappears on the doorstep, a frenzied look in her eye. She wildly scans the countryside for us. When she doesn't find what she's looking for, she takes off at a sprint in the direction of Carman's.

I follow her in the darkness with Dad hunched beside me as we steal across the fields. Carman's ceremonial fire glows in the distance with the same supernatural radiance of the night before. We duck behind one of the outbuildings to watch.

Carman raises her hands above the flames. She looks young and every bit the sorceress she promised to be, and I know at once that Clarissa and Amorin were telling the truth. My life force gave her energy. My life force made her young.

"Tonight is an evening of monumental change. No longer will we, the practitioners of Maleficium, remain in the shadows biding our time. The time has come to take what is ours."

My attention shifts to the objects she's holding.

"*Doo-loo, Foo-loo. Doo-la, Foo-lah,*" she chants as she releases the straw and the hair above the fire. The straw begins to dance from the heat. As its movement grows faster, my heart stops. Two men drag Scott from the barn I was in just yesterday. It wasn't a giant rat I heard, it was Scott. I was within an arm's reach of him, and I walked out. I could've saved him.

His feet begin to move on their own. His body jerks to the left and then to the right. My horror grows when I realize Scott's feet are moving to the beat of the straw above the fire.

Carman laughs in delight as the straw jerks and spins and Scott jerks and spins along with it.

"We will begin the evening with the sacrifice of a god to awaken the Fomorians."

Calliope rushes over to Carman, her hair wild. "We had a deal. I bring Gigi, and you promised Scott and Mark would not be harmed."

"You didn't fulfill your part of the bargain, did you? Where is this goddess you promised? Where is Mark? You didn't bring them."

She crashes to her knees in front of Carman. "I don't know where they are. When I got to the tower, they were gone. I don't know what happened to them. Carman, please. He's my son." She pulls at Carman's robes.

"I know he's your son, but he's also a god. A minor god, but a god nonetheless. The Fomorians will be pleased to receive Oegden, his Earth parents, and Brigit tonight. The sacrifice will bind them to me forever. I will become their master."

"His parents . . ." Calliope repeats before realization dawns on her. "You betrayed me. All this time you've treated me like a daughter. You promised me one day I would get my son back. We raised Alaric together. We were a family . . ." she trails off. "You used me."

"Calliope, dear, you came to me twenty years ago, bitter about the powers Brigit bestowed upon your sister. I showed you another way to power. You possessed such potential, but you fell in love with that poor excuse for a witch. More brains than ability. You. Left. Me. Remember? When Clayone sniffed you out, you betrayed your family and came groveling back to me. Here's a little secret," she says, putting her hand to the side of her mouth as if to whisper confidentially, "who do you think sent Clayone?"

"I left my son, my husband, because of you, you malevolent bitch." She spits at Carman's feet.

"A means to an end. Multiple sacrifices during the Super Blue Blood Moon on Samhain are necessary to enact my plan. This night was planned many moons ago. Now, onto our first sacrifice," she says raising her hands in the air.

The straw copies her movements and so does Scott, moving closer and closer to her, all the while his feet moving uncontrollably.

"Against my dead body, hag," Calliope shrieks, leaping in front of Scott.

"Very well. The order of sacrifice is incidental to the cause."

She begins chanting something that causes the flame to bend toward Calliope. Calliope knocks Scott to the ground and conjures a fireball out of the air. She whips it at Carman. Carman flicks it away as if nothing happened. Calliope throws another round of fire with one hand as she struggles to untie Scott's binding with the other.

Dad and I leap from behind the barn.

Carman throws back her head and laughs. "It's about time you two showed your faces."

My anger blurs my sight as I try to conjure fireballs of my

own, but nothing happens. Not one damn thing. I shove my hands into the ground and murmur to myself, hoping I can get vines to grow like I did in the tower, but again nothing happens.

I call the wind, but it does not respond.

Dad helps Calliope untie Scott. The rest of the coven crowd around them. They withdraw wands and swords from beneath their robes as if they were prepared for this battle all along. And maybe they were. Alaric told me Carman had the gift of sight. Maybe she saw this very moment.

Attack curses and counter spells fly in every direction. It is madness. It is chaos. It is death.

Carman's cackles rise above the din and confusion. My attention shifts back to her. I run at her, figuring that I can at least push her out of the way, but an invisible force stops me. I try again and again before I realize I can't move forward. I watch as the young mousy girl, Marie, stabs Calliope with a small dagger. The man who wanted revenge for his cheating wife keeps chanting a curse as he strikes both Dad and Scott with his fists over and over again. It's as if he has a thousand arms and is everywhere. I stare, powerless to stop it.

Carman watches me struggle with the invisible barrier. A cruel smile crosses her face.

"Is this amusing to you?" I hiss at her. "Are you afraid to fight me."

"Me, afraid to fight you? I am far more powerful than you will ever be. You are a poor excuse for a goddess. I was actually thinking about the surprise waiting for you."

"And what might that be?"

"Old Carman still has a few tricks up her sleeve. I've been preparing for this moment long before your grandmother's vision. Fifteen hundred years ago, I wanted to stand watch at Brigit's fire, but you wouldn't allow it because I had dabbled in the Dark Arts before coming to you. You told me I could not be saved. You said I was marked forever and one day would personally meet Derg instead of spending the afterlife in the Otherworld. You refused to forgive me, and it was that day I began devising my plan for your demise. To destroy you for destroying me."

Is Carman telling me that she's actually more than fifteen hundred years old? How many life forces has she sucked to keep alive?

"Let me get this straight. You've spent your entire life—fifteen hundred years—scheming a way to destroy Brigit?"

"Yes," she shrieks. "I worshipped you. I loved you. My entire childhood was spent dreaming that one day you would bless me with your presence, and then you reincarnated at Kildare. How was a sixteen-year-old learning the ways of the world to know that a little dark magic would destroy my chances of joining the Order of Brigit and presiding over your Flame? I made one mistake, and you couldn't see past it. You couldn't see my potential. I believed in you, and you destroyed me, so now I will destroy you!"

She throws something into the cauldron causing it to bubble over. A river of fire shoots twenty feet into the air then veers off toward me.

Two flashes of light burst from my hands, extinguishing the flames, before hurling off and blocking Dad, Scott, and Calliope from their attackers. The light expands, forming a shield in front of us. The rest of the coven members back away from the blinding radiance.

"Scott, Scott, are you okay?" I sprint over to him. I try to help him stand, but there's no indication that he's conscious, or even alive. "Scott, wake up! Don't you die on me. Don't you freaking dare."

He groans, and I know that whatever curse was laid upon him has been lifted. He tries to sit up but winces.

I tug on his arm. "Let me help you!"

"I'm right here. You don't need to shout."

"Always the pain in the ass. Even in a death match with a sorceress you manage to find your comedic side. Lucky us."

Dad helps Calliope to a standing position. Blood seeps from every part of their bodies.

"You can't win," Carman shrieks from the other side of the light. "The night isn't over."

A firebolt flies past my arm, narrowly missing Scott. I urge him on. We don't have time to find out what else Carman has in mind. Dad drags Calliope beside him, but their injuries are severe. They soon fall behind, but I can't worry about them right now. I need to get Scott—my brother, my best friend—away from Carman and her coven of twisted sorcerers. I tug him along, as fast as his damaged body will take him. When the screams of the fighting fade into the night and I can no longer see the flames, I slow down, suddenly feeling the absence of Dad and, by default, Calliope.

"Dad? Are you coming?" I shout.

When he doesn't answer, I glance around to make sure we weren't followed before I even consider leaving Scott to check on them. The familiar crumbled walls of the ruins give me hope. We're closer to Amorin's than I realized. We might have a chance after all. I ease Scott onto the laid stone.

"Scott? Scott, can you hear me?"

He makes no reply, but I can feel his chest weakly rising and falling.

"I need to help Dad. I'll be right back."

"And Mom . . ." he groans. "Don't forget Mom. Help her, please."

"I will," I promise him.

With the full moon to guide me, I retrace my path, searching for them. A few hundred paces or so away, I find their collapsed forms on the ground a few feet away from each other.

"Dad? Calliope?"

When neither one of them replies, I kneel over Dad and check for a pulse.

"Gigi, you need to get out of here. I'll be okay," he protests weakly.

"But I won't. Where are you hurt? Let me help you."

"How's Scott? Is he all right?"

"I think so. I'll do everything I can to fix him."

He smiles with his eyes closed. "I know you will, honey. I know you will. And Calliope?"

"Let me see." I crawl over to her. Her likeness is to Mom is uncanny except for the black hair. I bare her mark as well. "Calliope, can you hear me? Can you tell me where it hurts?"

She draws in a breath, and I know she's still alive, but who knows for how long. "Tell Scott, I'm sorry. My whole life has been about keeping him safe." Her body begins to seize. Her arms and legs jerk along with her torso until she goes still. A minuscule light exits her mouth, and her body goes slack.

"She's gone, isn't she?" Dad whispers.

"She is. I need to get you to Amorin's. I can help you there."

"When Maleficium of such magnitude is performed on a person, death is certain. No amount of magic, no matter how powerful, can undo the damage. Please go and protect yourself and your brother. Clayone could be out there."

"I can't leave without you."

"You have to . . ." he wheezes, gulping for air. "If not for yourself, for Scott. Please, Gigi."

I shake my head, refusing to listen.

"Please, Gigi, for me."

I nod in agreement.

He licks his lips. "I am so sorry I wasn't there for you as a father."

"Dad, you don't have to do this. I understand." I don't want him to strain himself any more than necessary.

"No," he whispers, shaking his head back and forth. "I am sorry that we put your protection above your need to be a child."

"Dad, you were there for me. You were there for everything—every birthday party, every recital, every holiday, every meeting with the principal."

He grunts. "But you didn't know who I really was. You deserved to know the truth."

"Dad, I think I did know. I think deep down I've always known. You were there for me—every time I needed a shoulder to cry on or someone to talk to . . . every time I needed a dad, you were there. You were always there. I love you." And the dam opens.

"I love you, Gigi. And Scott. Tell him how much I love him and how proud I am of the both of you. The two of you are destined to accomplish amazing things. Stories will be written of your greatness."

"Let's not get ahead of ourselves. Let's get through tonight. Let me help you stand."

"Gi, it's time to let me go. I love you both so much. Always remember that." He wheezes, then his frame falls still. His chest rises and falls, but barely.

"I will come back for you. I promise," I whisper to him because I'm not ready to let him go.

30

SURPRISE STALKING

*E*very ounce of my being wants to remain at Dad's side and save him. Bring him back from wherever he's gone to, but I must honor his wishes. I need to do that for him. Scott still needs me, and I promised Dad I would save him.

I leave his still frame, not knowing how much longer he has. Not knowing how much longer I'll need to ensure Scott's safety before returning to him. Not knowing if that will be fast enough. I command myself to return to Scott. Return to him and save him.

Never before have my footsteps been so heavy. Never before have I doubted so deeply if I can follow through with what I promised. But for Scott I'll try. I carry the weight of death—of all the deaths—with me. Every step is a miracle. "For Scott. For Scott," I chant to myself.

For no one else could I keep going.

There is no one else to keep going for.

I stumble over a few loose stones as I enter the ruins. I drop roughly to the cold, hard floor. Injury to myself is of little consequence. I search Scott for any indication he's still with me, but there's no sign of life. Not even a faint heartbeat. The final blow of his death crushes me to the unforgiving ground.

Lying in a state of complete and utter emptiness, too numb to feel the cold, too drained to mourn the loss, I stare at a small patch of shriveled black moss on the ruin's floor—as dead as I feel inside. No healing touch. No magical ability. Dead like everyone else in my life. I watch this lifeless piece of vegetation as a soft rain begins to fall. Green sparkles spread across the moss. Then slowly, ever so slowly, so slowly that I blink a few times to confirm that it's really happening and I'm not just seeing things, the moss turns to a brilliant shade of green. A green so bold and rich that I am reminded of another place. A place where time has no beginning and no end. If I can get to the fairy mound, I can return to the Otherworld and never feel again. Never feel pain. Never feel hurt or hope.

But hope is exactly what I begin to feel as I watch the dazzling patch of green on the stone floor. And love. I feel love. So much love. A warm fuzzy sensation grows within me as memories of Alaric rise to my consciousness—his lips dancing across mine, his strong arms embracing me, his mischievous smile, his intoxicating scent smelling of Mother Earth herself. I remember the way one of Gram's hugs felt like there was nothing in this world more important than me. My dancing sessions with my dad. The mutual love of friendship Lizzie and I shared. The joy I felt with Ryan's dedication to his friends and to Lizzie. The laughter and sibling love felt between Scott and me. Thousands of memories spin and weave within me, reminding me why I'm here. To feel pain. To feel hurt. To feel love. To remember what it's like to be human.

Flashes of every reincarnation come flooding back to me all at once along with the memories of the gifts I brought—

the love and the light. The healing. The inspiration. The magic. The joy. The hope. The hope I gave people. The hope that there was something greater than themselves. The hope that the sacrifices made today will be rewarded in this world or the next. The desolation I felt just moments ago is gone. Replaced with the realization . . .

I am Brigit.

A signal stone shifts, and I know I am no longer alone.

31

HEAR ME ROAR

I've tempted fate one too many times not to be surprised as the killer stalks toward me, but still I am. An ocean separated us. An *ocean* for god's sake. But still he's here. Ready to rip out my throat.

"I don't understand. How did you get here?" I whisper, mesmerized by the supernatural glow of piercing yellow eyes moving toward me in the darkness. I should run and scream or do something, anything rather than stand still and stare, but his presence freezes me in place.

"I've waited a long time for this moment," he rasps, his hot breath searing the edges of my hair.

"You were in the mountains around Clarissa's church in Vernal Falls. How did you get here? You weren't supposed to have the strength. My dad said you wouldn't have the strength."

"And how would your father know what the most powerful werewolf can or can't do? There is much you don't know about me, but I know who you are. I know about you . . ."

I pull back my shoulders and lift my chin. I am not afraid. I am a goddess. "You know nothing about me."

"Oh, I do. I know you never feel like you fit in, always the outcast because of a dead mother and no father to speak of. I know you constantly strive to prove yourself but always fall short."

"How could you know that?" I whisper.

"When I bit your friends, I read their minds. They became part of my pack—my all-knowing pack. They provided me with enough nourishment to shed my tomb—young prey, full of life and vigor—and then, when the moon was last full, I feasted on your grandmother. Her gifts were plentiful. She gave me the strength to carry me here, along with the imprint of your scent."

"You killed Gram? She didn't die of a heart attack?"

"Of course I did. The blood of Brigit coursed through her veins. She had many years left to live, but she is no longer. Soon you will join her for all eternity. Never to return to this world or the next. I will destroy you, and the curse on me and all of my kind will be lifted forever."

The rain that once gave me hope stops. A bitter, cruel wind blows the cloud cover away. The Super Blue Blood Moon illuminates the night sky with an eerie red glow, revealing Clayone, a grotesquely shaped form, half-man, half-wolf. He is twice the size of Ryan with haunting yellow eyes, long matted fur, and sharp canines dripping with saliva. He stands on his two hind legs, not fully-shifted, making him more terrifying than anything I've ever seen. But I cannot act like I'm afraid. He feeds on fear.

"Why do you believe I am the Goddess Brigit?"

"Because I can smell it," he snarls, edging dangerously close. A movement in the corner of my vision shifts my attention to Scott, his chest gently rising and falling. He's alive. Scott's alive. Albeit barely. But enough to give me hope.

Enough to give me courage. I am no longer afraid. I will do everything within my power to save him.

I am Gigi.

I am Brigit.

And together we will save him. My healing chalice is close. I can feel it. But I cannot get to it with Clayone here.

I embrace Gigi's strengths, and she has many.

"You can smell that I am the Goddess Brigit? Of course, I smell like her. I'm from her family line. No one can dispute my family tree. But to believe that I'm a goddess? You are sadly mistaken. In her last reincarnation, she left this world as pure as the day she arrived in it. I am far from pure. Light does not shine upon me."

"You lie."

"Do I? Or has Carman mislead you. You put your faith in the wrong person. So did I, and now everyone I love is dead. You've spent your entire life waiting for Brigit to reincarnate and just when you think you've found her, you're as far away from the truth as I am."

"I can smell her blood in your veins. You are Brigit!" he roars, pulling up to his full height.

"How do you know?" I ask again. "Because Carman told you? Because Calliope told you? Because of a little old prophecy? Come now, we both know anyone can make up a prophecy. They've both lied to you before. Why wouldn't they lie to you now?"

He hesitates, unsure what to make of my story. I take full advantage of his indecision. I edge toward the far wall.

"She told you Brigit was reincarnated, but she didn't tell you Oegden, her son, was. Why is that? Perhaps she's trying to protect him still by distracting you. From what I understand, Calliope and Carman are quite talented in the Dark Arts. They've even acquired the Vessel of Life to bring back the dead. Did you know that?"

The lies come easy now. They don't physically hurt like all the lies that came before. Maybe with my close proximity to death, my body has decided to stop fighting against me.

He steps toward me. "It makes no difference with the task before me."

Shit. That didn't go as I expected. Time to reshuffle the bullshit. "You didn't know, did you? Have you even spoken to Carman since you've returned?"

"No," he growls. "Is there a point to this line of questioning?"

Oh, there's a point all right.

"She's learned to manage the Dark Forces without the curse of the werewolf. Last I saw her she was preparing to summon the Fomorians—just think of the army she can assemble that wouldn't ever have to change shape. It's genius really. She distracts you with tales that I'm Brigit while she opens the portal to the Otherworld. Then, when her army is complete, she'll destroy you. She has no need for an ally limited by the moon."

"I won't be bound by the full moon once I kill you."

"She wants to rid the world of you."

"You lie!" he roars.

"Do I, or does she? Do you really want to take that chance? Where can I go tonight? The power of the Super Blue Blood Moon on the eve of Samhain is on your side to aid you, along with my scent imprint. I am defenseless against you. But Carman and Calliope also have the power of the tonight's moon. In just a short time, during the lunar eclipse, they'll lift the veil and summon a great army that will destroy you and all your disciples. You don't have much time. Tell me, are you prepared to battle the Fomorian army she plans to release?"

Again, he hesitates, unsure what his next move should be. He glances at the moon. The narrowest sliver of a shadow falls across the edge of it. He has maybe an hour to an hour and a half before the full lunar eclipse. Over the past few weeks, I've become something of an expert in the moon phases, just in case there was some truth to all the Goddess Brigit nonsense. It turns out there was.

He heaves several long breaths, and I know he's debating whether to kill me now or wait until the predestined time when the moon will be fully eclipsed and he has the most power to gain. He growls as he paces back and forth. He could easily just kill me now and be done with it. Finally he throws back his head and howls in rage before sprinting off into the night.

I stand in shock. I mean, I did offer a logical argument, but still, I never actually believed he'd leave me alone. The Fomorians must be truly horrific.

They are.

At least now when I hear voices in my head, I know it's my Brigit alter ego talking. That's a relief.

I approach a perfectly ordinary flat brown stone that looks like every other stone on the floor except for one small detail—tiny flecks of gold only visible in the moonlight or rain. It's a few feet away from the vault Amorin found this morning, but its contents are much different. I move the stone with a short incantation. *"Entrance to my Shrine, open to the one true Goddess."*

It magically shifts, revealing an opening in the floor and a stairway carved into the rock below.

"I'll be right back," I whisper to Scott and slip down into the opening. In a way, it's like I'm entering my own tomb, for I know the only way to trap Clayone away forever is to bind myself to him and seal ourselves inside forever. When we are bound, everyone I love, including all my people, will be safe, and I will perish for all time.

A radiant glow emanating from the stone stairs illuminates the way to my shrine. Nineteen nuns tended my Flame in this castle, and on the twentieth night, I tended it to keep the faith alive in my people. The new Flame will burn forever if I save Scott.

As I descend deeper into the shrine, even I, the Goddess Brigit, am amazed by the warmth permeating from the stone walls, the lack of dust and debris, the absence of rodent droppings or other signs of abandonment—almost like it's been awaiting my return. Eighteen nuns never knew about this shrine. The nineteenth—the only one of my flesh and blood—did. Clarissa has cared for it for all these centuries—even when the original Flame was extinguished, for which I cannot fault her. When I granted her the gift of immortality, I chose well. Carman forsook me the moment she did not receive her desired appointment as the nineteenth nun.

At the bottom, I follow a narrow passage and enter my shrine room on the right. Taking no notice of the gold ornamentation on the walls or the life-size statue of Brigit standing in the corner, I head directly to the stone alter and grab the ornate silver chalice before running back up the stairs. Scott hasn't moved, but he's still alive. I sense his life force.

Kneeling by his feet, I lift his left pant leg and remove the silver dagger from his ankle strap. The moonlight reflects off it as I drag the blade across my palm while chanting a healing incantation. I allow the blood to flow freely into the silver chalice. After a few drops have fallen, I place the dagger by Scott's side and raise the chalice to the moon in offering. I chant, *"From my blood, the Fallen shall be restored."* Once blessed, I bring it to his mouth.

"Scott, drink this please."

His lips open, and I pour the liquid down his throat. Suddenly, his breathing stops.

"Scott! Scott!" I shout, shaking him. "Scott, wake up. I

know you can hear me! Please Scott, wake up! Open your eyes! Scott, please!" I beg over and over, shaking him, but he won't respond. No sarcastic retort. No flippant remark. Nothing.

"Not Scott, please not Scott," I plead to the heavens above, holding him tightly against me. "You've taken everyone I love from me! Please just leave Scott. Don't take Scott. Please not Scott!"

A light rain begins to fall again. Wetness permeates my clothing, but it doesn't matter. I am as powerless against the elements as I am against everything while in human form. I am not some awe-inspiring goddess who unites the world for a common cause. I am not some all-knowing oracle who illuminates the path to knowledge for future generations. I am not a protector or a great healer. Without Scott, I am broken. Without Scott, I am nothing.

I took too long to realize I am Brigit, and now everyone I love is dead. They died for me. I couldn't save any of them. I took too long. I was too late.

"Too late," I sob. "I was too late." I wail into the moonlight, clutching my brother to my chest.

"I'm not supposed to be here by myself, all alone. It can't be over. It can't end like this. I can't be too late!" Tears stream down my face and I howl, not caring who hears me, not caring that Clayone may return any minute. "I'm sorry, so sorry," I cry burying my face in his chest.

"Sorry for what?" he mumbles.

I yank him to my chest. I can feel his life force returning to his limbs, his body, his soul. "You're alive! I can't believe it. It really worked," I cry into his hair. I saved him. I did it. I did what I wanted to do.

But before he can reply, before we can rejoice together, heavy, ragged breathing reeking of death fills the space between us. We both stiffen and pull away from each other to face our worst nightmare.

"What do we have here?" Clayone growls. "A joyful reunion?"

I glare at him, anger and hate replacing my happiness. "You're back."

He steps toward us. As much as I don't want to leave Scott, I shift away from him to put distance between us. Scott will not be a part of this death match.

As if by lunar pull, Clayone moves with me. "You tricked me into believing that Carman and Calliope were amassing an army to rise up against me. You made me question their purpose. Me, the most powerful being the world has ever known—the most powerful being the world will know—believing your lies."

"They're not lies," I growl.

He grunt-laughs. "Calliope's dead body is a hundred yards from where I stand . . ."

Scott collapses back into the stone.

". . . and Carman's fallen form lies across her alter on the brink of death. She's in no condition to release any Fomorians tonight. You are Brigit, and that is Oegden. I'll take care of him once I'm through with you. His powers haven't kept me down for thousands of years. His powers haven't made me a slave to the moon. But no more. Tonight I will have my revenge, and tomorrow the world will bow to me."

Carman was unharmed when we left the bonfire. What the hell happened? I don't know what's going on, but I don't have time to worry about it. I've got the Original Werewolf to vanquish.

I push myself off the ground. Feeling powerful. Feeling brave. "Ego trip much?"

Scott stares at me. *What are you doing?*

I smile. I've longed to hear his voice again—in person or

in my head—for weeks. I've missed him, I've needed him, and now I will protect him always.

Trust me.

"You've forgotten the prophecy, haven't you?" I ask Clayone as I step along the opening to my shrine and begin a wide circle that will include him. Without waiting for his response, I begin . . .

> *"One of love, one of light,*
> *Spring forth from the womb*
> *To guard from the night."*

As I chant the prophecy, I complete the first revolution around Clayone and put my plan into motion. Scott is alive. I've accomplished what I set out to do, and now I will bind Clayone in an unbreakable circle with me forever, my imminent death of little consequence.

> *"The power to heal. The power of youth.*
> *Their existence to all a living proof."*

Clayone's eyes follow me around as I complete my second rotation.

> *"As immortality weighs,*
> *One shall fall, one shall rise,*
> *To perish from all humankind.*

"You cannot destroy a god," I tell him as I finish my third counterclockwise rotation. "Belief is the very thing that gives us immortality. It's not the flesh and blood of a human. Shrines are dedicated to me. I have followers all over the world. Thousands come here every year because they believe in *me*. You have nothing. You are bound to the shadows because no one believes in you. No one knows your name, whereas I have a vast amount of power I can draw from." With a flourish of my arms, vines spring from the ground and rise up to me. "I would never have to become human again, and I would still have more power than you. Belief is what gives me power."

He steps toward me, causing me to briefly stop my first clockwise rotation. "You speak in riddles, but you won't be speaking for long. You don't believe in yourself. You don't believe you're Brigit. Your vines are merely parlor tricks."

"Don't I?" I resume my spell circle. "In the beginning, I admit I didn't believe. My family and friends gave me a weak sense of power because their belief in me was so strong, but when my brother was on his deathbed and I thought all was lost, I remembered who I was. I entered my personal shrine while you were gone. A shrine all but one knows exists. In there, I found the power I was lacking. I relinquished my mortality and now, before you, I am in full goddess form." I stand tall, lifting my arms for dramatic effect as I complete my second clockwise revolution. One more to go. "You cannot vanquish me anymore than you can destroy Oegden. See? Carman's assault on him had no effect. He is fully healed."

Scott tries to push himself up off the ground. He's still too weak to stand, but that won't stop him from trying to get to

Clayone to try to protect me. But it's my turn to protect him. He will not take this away from me.

Stay.

He claws across the ground toward Clayone and enters the perimeter of my circle. *No!* He shouts in my head.

He'll be locked in the circle with us if he keeps moving. *Get out!*

But he refuses to listen. He edges his way to Clayone who must either sense my distraction or the movement. He glances at Scott, then at me. A cruel smile crosses his face as he steps toward my brother.

"No!" I shout, frozen in place. I'm terrified that he'll do something to Scott, but if I break the circle now, I'll have to start over, and I don't think I'll get another chance to finish it before the full lunar eclipse is upon us.

Scott pulls the concealed dagger out and lunges at Clayone. Clayone shifts out of the way then rounds on Scott and kicks him clear across the ruins, far away from our circle. He lands with a thud. His body shudders from the impact, and his eyes slip shut.

His assailant throws back his head and calls to the blood red moon as it begins its final phase. The howl fills me with dread. It's coming.

I clear my throat. I need to work fast. "When you ran away, you allowed me to return to immortality."

He takes an aggressive step toward me. The opening to my shrine is the only thing separating us. A short leap for a werewolf his size, and I still have one final rotation to go before binding us in this circle for all time.

"No. You're spinning lies again."

The moon disappears, and I know time has run out, but I have to try anyway. Life as we know it depends on it.

"I speak not in falsehoods."

He reaches out one freakishly long arm and wraps his

claws around my throat, lifting me into the air. I close my eyes and send out a silent plea for divine assistance before it's too late.

I struggle to break free, batting at his arms, kicking at his legs, but my fight has no effect on him. He draws me to his rotting stinking canines dripping with anticipation. I kick at his balls—or where his balls should be. His nails tear into my neck as he drops me. I land hard, the wind knocked out of me. He lunges, his teeth leading the attack. I throw up my hands and squeeze my eyes shut. His teeth drag along my neck before he is knocked away by a force that comes out of nowhere.

Two large brown cows, their long hair weighed down with rain, hot air spiraling from their nostrils, plow him into the void with their long horns. I crawl to the edge, gasping for breath, and watch him fall. Surprise—the last look on his face.

I leap up and quickly shift the rock tablet back into position, step out of the circle, and complete my final rotation as I cast the spell that seals the vault for all time. No heir to Brigit will unwittingly open this one.

When I finish, I turn to Scott who's studying me closely. Color has returned to his cheeks, but I'm not sure if he can stand on his own.

He shakes his head at me.

"What?"

"Cows? Really? You bring cows to save me? That's the best you can do?"

"Brigit had two faithful brown cows for pets. These two are their descendants." I shrug my shoulders and receive a sandpaper lick as a thank you—or a you're welcome. I'm not sure which.

"You can't have something cool like dragons, or griffins, or at least unicorns?"

The other cow gives him a big sloppy kiss of his own.

"Ewww, gross," he screams as the cow shoves his wet nose into his face. "All right, all right, I guess cows can be pretty cool. Quit it, would you?" He shoves the head away as he tries to stand up. I dash over to help him, but he's already steadying himself on his new cow friend.

"So, what's with all the relinquishing your mortality? Did you actually do that? Is a goddess really standing before me?"

"I was trying to buy time with Clayone. I didn't have a clue how I was going to get rid of him. It's a good thing these cows showed up when they did, or we would have been doggy kibble."

If Scott had known my real plan, he'd be furious with me —always the big brother protecting his little sis.

"You know," he says, scratching his cow friend behind the ears, "I didn't hear them coming. You'd think with cows that big you'd hear their hooves on the stone. It's like they formed out of the mist."

"I've heard that the mist around here is very powerful."

"So, when did you realize you were the Goddess Brigit?"

I am not ready to admit to Scott or Dad or anyone else that I am the Goddess Brigit reincarnated—for reasons that are my own. "My big brother may not be the only storyteller in the family. Come on, let's go find Dad."

Scott's near-death experience was my breaking point. If his life hadn't been in peril, I would not have realized I was Brigit, I would not have discovered my shrine and recovered the healing chalice, and I would most certainly be dead.

I lie.

I cheat.

I steal.

I am a god.

32

TRUTHS REVEALED

*A*morin sits down on the bench next to me as I gaze into the remains of last night's bonfire.

"He's gone. I can't believe Dad's gone."

"He wanted it that way, dear," he says kindly. "He wanted to protect you. He thought maybe if he spoke to Calliope, he could convince her to help."

"Dad went to Calliope? He knew she was alive?"

He nods.

"Is that how Calliope found out where Scott was?"

"We think so. From what you told me last night about Carman, I believe she was the most highly skilled witch in Maleficium. There are stories about her that are centuries old. The fact that Calliope was her pupil raises considerable questions. Could they see that Clayone had been released, or did they somehow lead you and Scott into Clayone's prison? How long had Calliope been with Carman? Are there other students out there? With her centuries of scheming, it's doubtful she'd rely solely on Calliope. Where are the others? How did she intend to execute her plan? Did she succeed in releasing any Fomorians? Did she really die at her altar? Does she have any offspring?"

My head begins to ache as Amorin rattles off questions. When I raise my hand to my temples to relive the pain, he finally stops.

"I'm sorry, dear. Sometimes I get carried away. Our *family* has a tendency to do that."

The way he says "our family" causes me to turn to him in question. His eyes twinkle with mischief.

"You weren't just Dad's mentor, were you?"

He shakes his head. "I was also Rose's mate."

"I thought he died in a plane crash."

He smiles at me. "He didn't, but her prophecy scared her. Even without the gift of sight, her powers far surpassed most witches, as do mine. We decided it was safest to keep our magic separate. It was bad luck that Calliope came here and met Carman instead of me. But darkness attracts darkness."

My family have always put the life of Brigit above their own happiness, but I can bring him some joy now.

"Gramps?"

"I prefer 'Granda' or 'Daddo,' but you can call me whatever you'd like."

I wrap my arms around him.

"Ah, I see we are no longer keeping secrets from Gigi," Clarissa says, sitting on the bench across from us.

"You're not related to me too, are you?"

"I am from Brigit's family tree, but my line stopped with me. I'm glad there won't be any more secrets though. I followed your father's wishes, but I believe in full disclosure."

I stare at her.

"What is it you want to ask, dear?"

"Clarissa, why didn't my magic work last night? I was completely powerless."

"You possess a tremendous amount of magic, dear. More

magic than I've ever witnessed. But your magic is a green magic. It's noncombative. You can restrain an aggressor and resist curses through shields both visible and invisible. You can imprison your aggressor, but you cannot harm him or her. When anger replaces reason, green magic will not work. And remember, child, you are Brigit—harming any living creature, good or bad, is against your nature. That's why Scott had to shoot your friend Ryan. You can't fire a gun. That's why the cows came. They answered your call. And if you had succeeded in binding Clayone to you, you would've been completely defenseless against him."

I gaze into her clear blue eyes and feel at peace.

"You were going to bind yourself to Clayone?" Scott walks into the garden. "Really? That's what you came up with? You're the Goddess Brigit, and you were just going to throw your life away."

I shrug my shoulders.

"Why would you do that? You still have your whole life ahead of you."

"You were safe. Nothing else mattered."

"Come here, you dimwit," he says, yanking me off the bench and into his arms. My heart fills with love as I think of my brother and everything he means to me. What we mean to each other. I can handle anything with him by my side.

A loud clap of thunder pulls us apart. Dark clouds blot out the sun. I pull away from him and look from Clarissa to Granda. "We aren't done, are we?"

Scott's shoulders stiffen. "Aren't done with what?"

"No, we aren't," Granda says.

Clarissa stares up the sky. "A terrible storm is on the horizon. The battle has only begun."

"Battle? What do you mean battle?" Scott says.

"The real reason you and Gigi are here."

"Real reason? I thought we were here to destroy Clayone."

"Clayone's death was easy," Granda says.

"You call last night easy?" I ask as another clap of thunder signals the fast-approaching storm.

"Gigi, child," Granda says, "last night was easy. We expected much higher casualties."

"Brigit reincarnates only when her people are in real danger. No one was in real danger last night," Clarissa says.

"I think my mom and dad would disagree with you," Scott says. "Who are you anyway?" The muscles feather across his jaw.

"Scott, meet Clarissa Radley. *The* Clarissa Radley. And I hate to say it, but I think she might be right. During my Otherworld visit, Gram gave me this." I withdraw the bundle of herbs from my pocket.

Scott picks it up and sniffs it. "What is it?"

"I believe it's nightlock. Brigit's third spell against the werewolf."

Clarissa nods at Granda. "Children, there's another prophecy."

"Of course there is," Scott says.

THE END

Reviews are like dance parties. Sometimes awkward, sometimes spastic, but someone's got to get them started!

Keep reading for an excerpt of
Dark Moon: The Goddess Chronicles Book Three

JOIN THE KOVEN

Read Clarissa and Carman's origin story, The Druids Sisters of the Gallicennial, FREE by signing up for K's Koven. Be the FIRST to find out about new releases from Best-Selling Author, K.B. Anne. PLUS, receive Newsletter Subscriber Only Bonus Content, insight on Celtic Mythology, Druids, Witches, Werewolves, and Magic, and so much more! Join K's Koven today!

ABOUT THE AUTHOR

Evil author person causing book hangovers since 2018. Known to erupt into malevolent laughter fits while she writes urban fantasy featuring fierce females, swoon worthy heroes who actually listen, and explosive action because everyone needs excitement in their lives.

She writes the best-selling urban fantasy series, *The Goddess Chronicles* and *The Silver Fae* Series. She has a thing for drool worthy wolf shapeshifters. Who doesn't?

She lives in Northeast PA with 3 goblins, a task master, 2 hell hound overlords, and 2 unicorns—though sadly they don't fart rainbow glitter. The Goddess Chronicles and Silver Fae Series are ready for your consumption. Warning: May cause book hangovers.

Visit her website for more information or to contact her at kbanne.com.

Contact info:
www.KBAnne.com
kim@kbanne.com

facebook.com/KBAnneWrite
twitter.com/KBAnneWrite
instagram.com/KBAnneWrite

ALSO BY KB ANNE

The Goddess Chronicles (COMPLETE)

Wide Awake: The Goddess Chronicles Book 1

Blood Moon: The Goddess Chronicles Book 2

Dark Moon: The Goddess Chronicles Book 3

Shadow Moon: The Goddess Chronicles Book 4

Oak Moon: The Goddess Chronicles Book 5

Storm Moon: The Goddess Chronicles Book 6

The Goddess Chronicles Books 1-3 Boxset

The Goddess Chronicles Books 4-6 Boxset

The Silver Fae Series (COMPLETE)

Throne of Silver: Silver Fae 1

Silver Fae Hunter: Silver Fae 2

Heirs of Wings and Shadows: Silver Fae 3

Court of Wings and Shadows: Silver Fae 4

Crown of Flames: Silver Fae 5

DARK MOON: THE GODDESS CHRONICLES BOOK THREE

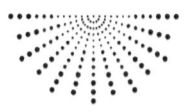

BESTSELLING AUTHOR
K.B. ANNE

DARK
MOON

THE GODDESS CHRONICLES - BOOK THREE

THE SECOND PROPHECY

Bound by blood, yet split by purpose—
    Dead but not gone.
    Hunger quenched only by death.
    Contained but not restricted,
    Controlling that once dedicated to another.
    The Storm approaches.
    Enemies emerge through stealth of step,
    Led by one with two faces.
    Force alliance,
    Or expire from unstoppable force.

NEW DRAMA

The fairy mound looks so ordinary from Alaric's thinking rock. There's little indication of the wonders awaiting on the other side of it. The vibrant greens. The brilliant blues. Mom. Gram. Maybe even Dad by now. I might be a reincarnated goddess but that doesn't mean I've been downloaded with all the information I'll ever need to know about the admission process to the Otherworld. In fact, it's the complete opposite. Last night, after the cows plowed Clayone into the depths of my shrine, one of them licked my cheek. With that sandpaper kiss, Brigit's memories were wiped away with it. Leaving just me, Gigi Brennan, a girl who lies. Who cheats. Who steals. A girl of no exceptional worth or value, whose family gave their lives so that she might live.

And if the allure of seeing my family again wasn't enough of a temptation, the faint scent of honey blossoms and the whispers of fairy wings try to trick me into visiting. But I know if I return to the Otherworld anytime soon, I'll remain there forever, and I have far too much living to do in this one first. I owe Gram, Mom, and Dad a long, full life.

I rub my new crystal necklace back and forth across my

lips. Clarissa gave it to me this morning. Most likely as a bribe because she wouldn't let me go with her, Amorin, and a few of the other coven members to Carman's bonfire to take care of last night's fallen. It's not that I possess some fascination with rotting Maleficium witch corpses, but I wanted proof that Carman was dead and that the entire evening wasn't a result of a grossly overactive imagination. But when I asked Clarissa if I could go, she insisted I stay with Scott while he recovered from his wounds. I tried to argue with her. I might have even added in some I'm-a-goddess-don't-you-want-me-to-be-happy? whining, but she manipulated me into doing exactly what she wanted. She wasn't above using Scott as a carrot—I admired her approach.

When she gave me the necklace, she told me the crystal along with the ring of amethyst stones would soothe me with their calming properties and alleviate my grief and sadness. I told her a few stones wouldn't fix what's wrong with me—because I'm a freaking shit show. Just because I'm a reincarnated goddess doesn't mean I can't be a bitch too. She gave it to me anyway.

I suppose, in a way, the necklace did help me this morning. It distracted me while they were gone and Scott was sleeping. I studied the crystal and the amethysts in the sunlight, searching for imperfections. I didn't find any. Then I focused my energy into it to see if I could make it glow. I couldn't, but it passed the time. After a few hours, I grew restless and ornery. Amorin sensed as much when he returned from the bonfire site. He suggested I go for a walk and stretch my legs. That's how I ended up at the fairy mound thinking about everyone I lost to a psychotic, over-sized werewolf and a power-hungry, revenge-bent witch. Amorin, or Granda—it's still feels weird to call him that when I only recently discovered I had a mom and dad who actually cared about me—alluded to another prophecy, the real reason why Scott and I reincarnated. I can't imagine a fight more devastating and emotionally draining than the one we barely survived last night. With the exception of Scott, everyone I love is dead. How could things get worse?

"Why does my siofra continue to carry such heavy burdens?" Alaric's enchanting baritone voice calls out to me. His beautiful, dancing, emerald-green eyes remind me of the Otherworld—vivid and full of life. The moment his lips meet mine, my fears and worries magically disappear. At Metropol all those weeks ago, I blacked out after we kissed. Whether because of him or because I'd unknowingly taken something, I don't know. But each kiss since then strengthens me. It's like he gives me energy when everyone else seems to take it away.

Eventually, he pulls back, dazzling me with his deliciously mischievous smile and sparkling white teeth.

"I missed you," he whispers, inhaling deeply. "I told you I'd come back to you. I will always come back to you. I will always find you. You believe me, don't you?" he murmurs, his eyes intense.

Content to bask in his attention, I smile back at him. "Uh-huh," I manage to reply, sounding like the dimwit Scott likes to call me and not the goddess I am.

He brushes a lock of my hair behind my ear. "I came straight to you. I didn't even stop at home because I couldn't wait to see you. I have good news."

For some reason chills run down my spine, as if I somehow know that what he's about to tell me is going to be bad. "Go on," I whisper reluctantly when he doesn't continue.

"Right before I left, Nan told me my dad was coming home. I want you to meet him. I want you to be a part of my life."

I extract myself from his hold, breaking whatever spell we cast together whenever we touch. I turn away to face the fairy mound. A pit roots in my stomach. There are many things I know about his nan and his "aunt," Calliope, that he doesn't know—or at least I don't think he does. If he knew they wanted me dead, he wouldn't have left me yesterday. He might have been raised by them, he might even be dedicated to them, but I believe with all my being that his feelings for me are stronger. That being said, this new piece could be the surprise Carman warned me about. I hate surprises—especially if they have anything to do with psychos of any kind.

"How long has your dad been gone?"

He embraces me from behind, nuzzling my neck. "Fifteen years."

My heart speeds up, my vision blurs, and I suspect I begin to lose the ability to speak, but my next question is much too important not to ask.

"What's your dad's name?"

"Clayone."

The edges of consciousness slip away.

"Gigi? Gigi! Are you okay?"

I find myself cradled in Alaric's arms, his warmth permeating my soul, making me better, stronger, at peace. Making me hate myself more than I already do for being so weak. Screw the damsel-in-distress routine. I need to get my blood sugar checked. I can't pass out every freaking time something shocking happens—especially since something shocking occurs daily. Next time it might not be someone who cares about my well-being catching me.

And I have to believe that Alaric cares about me. Despite who I am. Despite who he is.

"What did you say your father's name was?" I hope beyond reasonable, rational hope that I heard him wrong as a result of someone shoving cotton balls in my ears when I wasn't paying attention.

"Clayone."

Cold certainty wraps around my heart. I shrink into myself and roll out of his grip and into a standing position. I *was* firm in my belief that he cared for me more than he cared for his nan or his "aunt." But this new reveal, this blasted surprise from Carman, could ruin us.

His hands curl around my biceps from behind. For the first time in his presence I realize how very breakable I am. I command myself not to shudder from his touch. My body, however, ignores my warnings.

"Gigi, what's wrong?"

I pull away from him. "I'm not feeling well. I need to go home."

He rushes over to me. "Let me help you. You look terrible."

I drop my eyes. I can't look at him. I want to, but I can't. It's devastating that the one person, the first person I finally feel something for, might be the one most terrible for me. The one whose father wanted to kill me so I imprisoned him for all of eternity instead.

He draws me into a tight embrace. My initial, natural impulse allows me to sink into him. Then my brain reminds me why I can't. Why I shouldn't. I break away and start cutting across the meadow toward Granda's cottage and either a psych evaluation or a straitjacket. "I got it. It's not far."

He easily catches up to me and swings his arms around me as if to carry me. I try to resist, both frustrated that he thinks I can't walk on my own and also that I can't let him. I can't let myself care for him more than I already do. I swat at him, but he completely ignores my effort and sweeps me off my feet.

"Alaric, I'm fine. Let me walk."

He's the only one who has purposely held me when I

could actually move by my own power—first at Carman's and now here. Scott, Ryan, and random strangers have carried me when I wasn't completely coherent, but Alaric possesses some impulsive need to cart me around. The quirk endears him to me even more, which given the current circumstances is unfortunate and potentially hazardous to any long-term living goals I might have. My head, with a mind of its own and possibly a death wish, rests on his chest.

"Better?" he asks, his voice like a cat's purr.

I tell myself to forget about the potential future drama and conflict that is bound to occur between us and soak in this feeling of security and comfort, because inevitably, in the end, it'll all go to shit. Why should the fact that I now know I'm a goddess be any different?

"Everything all right, Gi?"

He can either read my mind—which I pray to the gods he can't—or he can read my body language, which at least doesn't indicate that a war was waged last night and his family lost. My family lost too, but in a much different way.

I nod, afraid that my voice will betray me. He pulls me in closer, as if sensing I need comfort. Maybe he does too.

All too soon our time together comes to end. We wind up at Granda's faster than I would have if I had walked on my own two feet. He lets himself into the front gate with me still cradled in his arms. The gate creaks behind us, but it's not the noise it makes that alarms me—it's my enraged brother stalking down the path.

"Who the hell are you?" he growls.

Alaric's arms tighten. "I can ask you the same."

"I'm her brother. Put her down."

His tension eases, but it still boils just below the surface. "Brother? Gi never mentioned her brother was here."

Scott stops in front of me. "She never mentioned you either. Now, unhand her."

"Oh my god, Scott. 'Unhand her'? What are you, an Arthurian knight returned from the dead?"

He glares at me. *Quiet.*

I haven't even gotten started yet.

"I said, put her down," he hisses.

I glare at him. "And I said, I'm not done yet."

He scowls at me in return. *You realize you just admitted you can read minds.*

"I've done no such thing." Then I realize I have, but it's too late to cover up my mistake. "Alaric, would you mind setting me down now?"

He obliges, which is also surprising. Most people don't listen to me, let alone honor my requests. Well, except for Granda's coven, but only when I act goddess-like, not when I'm just Gigi. I cross my arms and stare at Scott. He can be a downright bastard when he wants to be.

Alaric rests his hands on my shoulders. It makes him seem like he's on my side. That he'll always be on my side, regardless of the secrets I keep from him.

"Scott, Alaric. Alaric, Scott. Now, play nice."

Alaric reaches a hand over to Scott, palm out. Scott scowls at me again before extending his. If he keeps up the constant facial disapproval, he'll get wrinkles deeper than the Grand Canyon. Would serve him right too.

There are firm handshakes and then there are iron death-grip handshakes. I watch as veins and tendons strain and knuckles whiten. Before any bones break, I rest my hands on top of theirs. Their grips soften immediately. At least I retained some of the Goddess Brigit's healing touch, or maybe the crystal and amethysts actually work.

"There, there. Now let's make peace."

Scott rolls his eyes and releases his grasp. "Nice to meet you, Alaric."

"Likewise," Alaric says, returning his hand to my shoulder.

The three of us stand in an awkward testosterone-filled silence.

"Scott, I'd like to speak to Alaric for a minute."

"Sure," he says.

"Why don't you go inside, and I'll meet you in there?"

His arms return to their crossed position. "I'll wait."

I raise my eyebrows. "I'd like to speak to him a-*lone*."

He growls, "Fine," and stomps up the path and into the cottage, leaving the front door open so he can eavesdrop. He's un-freaking-believable.

I turn to face Alaric.

A touch of accusation sparks his pupils. "You didn't mention your brother was here."

I'd like to be as up-front and honest as possible with Alaric because there are already far too many secrets between us. I also don't want to send him home to an empty house—or worse—to the fallen remains of his nan and his aunt in case Granda and Clarissa left them at the bonfire site. But I need to figure some things out. A lot of things. Like is Alaric really Clayone's son? And if so, is he a werewolf? And if so, will he want to kill me too? You know, run-of-the-mill teenage drama.

But I ignore those nagging concerns and reach for his hands to pour good-vibe energy into them. "He just got here yesterday."

"And he already got into a fight. Not surprising, given his bad attitude."

Even without being able to read his mind, I know he means the bruises covering most of Scott's face. Unfortunately, it was much worse than a fight. It was a battle between life and death. But it's the wounds Alaric can't see that are the real cause of worry.

"He's protective of me."

Alaric stiffens. "Did someone mess with you when I was gone?"

I reach up and wrap my hands around his neck to pull his lips to mine. "He's not the only one protective of me."

He smiles before our lips meet.

Quit it. Scott pours all his focus into making me hear his single thought.

Of course, I ignore him.

"Ahem," he clears his throat.

I break away and turn to him. "Really? Privacy, please."

"We need to talk *now*," he says.

"In a minute."

Right now.

"Fine."

Alaric looks from me to the open door where Scott is standing and back to me. "Do you two read each other's minds?"

I pull away from him. I forget myself when we're together. "What? That's weird. No. Just brother-sister ESP."

He dips down in front of me, studying my reaction. "Are you sure? Because I only heard part of the argument, but it seems decisions were made."

His powers of observation will only add to the trouble.

"Would you mind leaving and maybe meeting at our secret spot later?"

He eases back into me. "And finish what we've been trying to start."

I wink as I step away. "Something like that. Meet at say . . . nine."

"Brilliant. Leave your brother at home."

I glance up at Scott who's been shouting in my head for the past several seconds. "Make it ten, and that shouldn't be a problem."

A little sleeping potion never hurt anyone.

"Until then, sweet Gigi," he says, leaning down for another kiss.

My insides turn to mush, which I never thought would be possible. I assumed my organs were made of granite and vinegar along with a heavy dash of toxic sludge. "Until we meet again," I murmur as our lips find each other once more.

To keep reading, grab your copy today...

Dark Moon: The Goddess Chronicles Book 3

THRONE OF SILVER: SILVER FAE BOOK ONE

CHAPTER ONE

*D*ive in.

That was the advice the swim team captain gave me when I gingerly dipped my toe in the pool at my first 5:30 a.m. swim practice three years ago. You see, the cold shocks your body into action. Stroke after stroke, you concentrate on your breathing, and the angle of your arms as they reach and pull through the water, and the height and depth of your kick, rather than on the freezing temperatures —at least that's the idea anyway.

Dive in.

I took that advice to heart. Made it my life's mantra, really.

So, when Sami texted me about a summer fellowship at Trevnor University's Leadership Academy, I begged her to pick me up an application. I couldn't think of a better way to spend June, July, and August than adding Summer Fellowship to my Georgetown application. My early acceptance was all but guaranteed.

But the entrance exam was tomorrow, at the tail end of

my post-season training for States, and in the midst of planning prom, Spring Fling, and our junior class trip, plus track started Monday.

Dive in.

My mantra sometimes got me in over my head.

CHAPTER TWO

*L*aughter exploded around me as I hurried through the school's front entrance. Over by the water fountain, four seniors played Hacky Sack while an audience of giggly underclassmen watched, making noises accentuated with rounded oohs and angled aahs. They all probably went to last night's basketball game too—the lucky bastards. While I discussed table linens and canapés with hotel managers, they got to watch the Webster Titans trounce the Bay Cardinals, 90-40.

Sometimes I hated these classmates of mine.

I mean *really* hated them.

None of them had two hours of swim practice this morning. None of them had two meetings during school, another meeting after school, followed by two more hours of swim practice. None of them had a To Do list so complicated and involved, even I knew it wouldn't be completed until after graduation.

Sometimes I wondered what it would be like not to worry about tomorrow, or next week, or next year. To live in the moment and just *be.*

A long stream of water hit me square on the nose.

Or not...

Shocked gasps ping-ponged through the ten-foot wide, locker-lined hallway, followed by an awkward, collective silence.

My body flickered—it had been doing that a lot lately especially when I got mad or annoyed about something. It felt like ocean waves slamming against my chest, and no matter how strong a swimmer I was, sometimes the big ones knocked me on my ass even when I was only knee deep.

I took a few deep breaths to calm myself. Thankfully, the flickering stopped. I was never standing in front of a mirror when it happened so I didn't know if the flickering was something other people saw or it was just in my head—which concerned me on a number of levels, but I couldn't worry about any of that right now. Someone needed to be punished for their crime.

I tracked the gaze of the surprised onlookers. My assailant, an underclassman with an unsteady grip on a green squirt gun, shook in his red Nike sneakers. I wiped my face and flicked the water in his direction. The droplets soared through the air and landed on his flushed, round cheeks. To his credit, he took it like a man, but unfortunately for him, he became the target of the dark, foul mood that descended upon me the moment I stepped into school.

"Don't you have a place you need to be?"

"Y...yes, sssorry Starrrr," he said, adding an overflowing consonant stream in the already crowded hallway. I narrowed my eyes. He tossed the squirt gun into the garbage can and sprinted away, red Nikes and all. When the plastic toy landed at the bottom of the can, it was as if someone hit play and all the students returned to their regularly non-scheduled lives.

Yep, today, I *definitely* hated them.

I stomped through the crowds, throwing the occasional elbow and the well-directed shove, because evidently, I was still the only one who needed to be somewhere.

Frank's buzzed head towered over the sea of students. I caught a glimpse of tight red ringlets by his side and understood why he didn't wait for me after practice.

He glanced down the crowded hall. A broad smile crossed his face the moment he saw me. One icy vein thawed. "Hey Starr," he said, then winked at the redhead. "I'll see *you* later."

"Bye Frankie," she replied, smiling like she just won the boyfriend sweepstakes. Frank was the total package—tall, dark, handsome with the brains and personality to match, but he wouldn't date Little Red long enough for her to find out. He went through girls faster than he swam the fifty, and he held the school record in that.

I frowned at him. "Frankie?"

He shrugged.

I spun my combination into my locker. "She already has a nickname for you?"

He smirked.

I tried my combo again, but my locker refused to cooperate. It was like it wanted to add further insult to injury.

At least in this case, I could cause bodily harm to it without being frowned upon. I kicked the base of the locker since my foul mood hadn't completely lifted and kicking metal seemed like a productive means to releasing frustration. Plus I didn't know what was up with the whole body flickering thing. I wasn't even sure if I wanted to mention it to my best friend.

Frank rested his hands on my shoulders and guided me to the side. He hit the locker just below the locking mechanism, and it popped open. He smiled as he rested against the locker next to mine. "When you got it, you got it."

I rolled my eyes.

"You know, I'm considered quite a prince to every girl in this school but…" He zeroed in a finger on my nose.

I swatted it away. "I know how charming you can be. The entire female population of Roger G. Webster High knows how charming you can be."

He closed the distance between us. "I can't help it if girls find me irresistible, but my dating days would come to an end if you went out with me."

Most girls would love the attention Frank gave me. *Most* girls would grow red-faced and faint if they heard half the come-ons he practiced on me. *Most* girls haven't been best friends with him since he was a short, obnoxious, hormone-ridden, scrawny seventh grader who wore ratty yellow Sponge Bob t-shirts and couldn't get a date to save his life.

I shoved him into class. "Get a grip."

To keep reading, grab your copy of Throne of Silver: Silver Fae Book One